ORANGE
for the
SUNSETS

ORANGE

for the

SUNSETS

TINA ATHAIDE

 KATHERINE TEGEN BOOKS

An Imprint of HarperCollins Publishers

Katherine Tegen Books is an imprint of HarperCollins Publishers.
Orange for the Sunsets
Copyright © 2019 by Tina Athaide
All rights reserved. Printed in the United States of America.
No part of this book may be used or reproduced in any manner whatsoever without written permission except in the case of brief quotations embodied in critical articles and reviews. For information address HarperCollins Children's Books, a division of HarperCollins Publishers, 195 Broadway, New York, NY 10007.
www.harpercollinschildrens.com

Library of Congress Cataloging-in-Publication Data

Names: Athaide, Tina, author.
Title: Orange for the sunsets / Tina Athaide.
Description: First edition. | New York, NY : Katherine Tegen Books, an imprint of HarperCollinsPublishers, 2019] | Summary: In alternating voices, friends Asha and Yesofu, one Indian and one African, find their world turned upside-down when Idi Amin decides to expel Asian Indians from Uganda in 1972.
Identifiers: LCCN 2018021529 | ISBN 978-0-06-279529-8 (hardback)
Subjects: | CYAC: Friendship--Fiction. | Social classes--Fiction. | Ethnic relations--Fiction. | East Indians--Uganda--Fiction. | Family life--Uganda--Fiction. | Forced migration--Uganda--Fiction. | Amin, Idi, 1925-2003--Fiction. | Uganda--History--1971-1979--Fiction. | BISAC: JUVENILE FICTION / Historical / Africa. | JUVENILE FICTION / Social Issues/ Friendship. | JUVENILE FICTION / People & Places / Africa.
Classification: LCC PZ7.1.A887 Or 2019 | DDC [Fic]--dc23 LC record available at https://lccn.loc.gov/2018021529

Typography by Laura Eckes
19 20 21 22 23   CG/LSCH   10 9 8 7 6 5 4 3 2 1
❖
First Edition

To my mum and brother, Steve.
And Daddy, in the words of Winnie the Pooh,
you may be gone from my sight, but you
are never gone from my heart.

ENTEBBE, UGANDA

1972

DURING THE SUMMER of 1972, the president of Uganda—Idi Amin—had a dream.

God spoke to him and told him to kick all foreign Indians out of Uganda.

Word of his dream spread throughout the country.

It reached the ears of best friends—Yesofu and Asha.

He was African.

She was Indian.

Asha had lived in Uganda her whole life.

They weren't worried.

1

YESOFU

YESOFU GLANCED AT his watch. Nine o'clock. He'd promised Mamma he'd be back no later than nine thirty. "*Yanguwa!*" she'd called to him as he ran out the door. Of course. She wanted him to hurry up. It was mostly dark now except for the light spilling out the windows of the Entebbe Institute. From what Yesofu could tell, only a couple of people were still inside. He stepped back into the shadows of the banyan tree and waited. The band announced it was their last song for the night and started howling like McCartney and Lennon.

They say it's your birthday.
We're gonna have a good time.

They sounded almost as good as the Beatles. Yesofu tapped his foot and sang along. He stepped forward and peered through the thick branches. Inside he saw Asha jumping around, her arms in the air and a big smile on her face. Her twelfth birthday party was all she'd talked about for the past few months. Yesofu pulled out the crumpled card from his pocket. It was the first invitation he'd ever gotten from her. He'd thought about going . . . wanted to go, even up until last night, but then he remembered Mamma's words.

You and Asha are from different worlds.

She'd said it in Luganda, their Ganda tribal language that she used when she meant business.

He got it. Asha, she was oblivious. Didn't get how him being African and her Indian made them different. It was the whole reason he wasn't at her party right now. The Indian club accepted African members, but the only Africans inside were the club boys serving the drinks and food. It would have felt weird, him being at the party. Problem was, he shouldn't have told Asha he'd go.

The wind whispered through the tree branches and Yesofu shivered. Misambwa—the wood and stream spirit. Being Christian didn't change his beliefs. Ganda people knew not to go to the water well or into the woods to collect twigs at certain times of the day. Only Yesofu was standing outside the Indian club. Surely Misambwa wouldn't show up here. Yesofu glanced up into the thick canopy of leaves and branches. He'd wait a couple more minutes. Better not to chance things and anger the spirits. The doors opened and Asha stepped outside. Finally. Yesofu moved into the light and waved.

"Asha!"

She looked up and walked over. "What are you doing here?" She crossed her arms and glared at him.

"Happy birthday!" He raised his hand for a high five, but she stood with her arms tightly knotted. This wasn't going to be easy.

"I got you something." He reached into his pocket and pulled out a yellow, slightly crumpled sachet. Green string was wrapped around the edges and tied into a messy knot. Yesofu pressed it into Asha's hand. "*Furahia siku ya kuzaliwa,*" he said. Birthday wishes sounded better in Swahili.

Excitement flickered in Asha's brown eyes. Wait until she saw what was inside. No way could she stay mad. Her fingers tightened around the sachet. Had she guessed? Yesofu wished she would hurry.

Asha pressed her thumb against the wrapping. She pulled at the string and then stopped. "What's wrong?" Yesofu asked.

She looked at him and shoved the gift back into his hand. "I don't want it."

"Come on . . . open it."

"No."

"Then I'll do it." Yesofu tugged open the knot, pulled apart the paper, and held up a string of round beads. The brown, orange, blue, and red colors shined in the moonlight. A friendship bracelet. Nearly all the girls in their class had one. A bracelet exchanged with your best friend.

There was no way he'd be caught wearing a beaded bracelet. What would the guys on the cricket team say? But Asha could.

Asha's fingers fidgeted, tugging at the hem of her sleeve. She was pretending not to care, but he could tell she wanted to try it on. Yesofu jiggled the bracelet—*try me on. Try me on*—

The beads softly clinked. She looked at the bracelet and rubbed her bare wrist, but still, she didn't reach for it.

"Why didn't you come to my party?" Asha asked. "Neela and everyone said you wouldn't, but I didn't listen. I said you would . . . and you made me look like a fool."

"I wanted to. I did." Yesofu dropped his arm, the bracelet dangling from his hand. "I even came tonight, but then . . . I couldn't. You. Me. We're different."

"It's never mattered before. Who cares?"

"Everyone!" said Yesofu. "Your friends. Our parents. And me. I care. I'm not like you. My family *works* for your family."

"So what?" Asha stepped forward and poked Yesofu in the chest. "You're my friend. You should have come."

4

Yesofu looked at Asha and something inside him shifted. He wasn't her houseboy to order around. He grabbed her arm and tried to shove the bracelet onto her wrist. "Here, take it."

"Let go!" Asha snatched her hand out of Yesofu's grasp.

SNAP!

The string broke. The beads dropped—one by one—falling in the open space between him and Asha, disappearing into the dirt and grasses. The empty string dangled from his hand.

"I—I—I'm so sorry—" stammered Asha.

Yesofu chucked the string at her. His heart pounded as he scrambled onto his bike. He took off, pedaling faster and faster until everything around him was a blur.

"Wait!" he heard Asha call out. "Yesofu!"

He blocked her voice with images.

The times he'd had to come through the back door at Asha's house.

The times he'd stayed in the kitchen when her parents had guests over.

The hours he'd spent in the sugarcane fields to pay for the beads.

It was like he was seeing his life for the first time, and he didn't like it.

≥ 2 ≤
ASHA

AFTER MORNING MASS, Asha raced home ahead of Mama and Papa. She normally liked attending church with the other Catholic Indians from South India, but today she couldn't stop thinking about Yesofu. Back in her room, she traded her Sunday dress for the *salwar kameez* that lay crumpled on the floor, and scooped the three beads off her nightstand. She'd been rotten to Yesofu last night. She'd seen the hurt on his face and the way he'd taken off like he couldn't get away fast enough. What had the priest said in his sermon?

Think before you act.

Your anger will pass, but your actions will remain.

If only she'd taken the bracelet. How hard would it have been to thank Yesofu and put it on her wrist? It sounded easy.

6

But last night, all she could think about was how he'd lied about coming to her party. She took a deep breath, pushing down the anger starting to rise. That was the reason she was in this mess right now. Focus, Asha. Find the beads and fix the bracelet. That would put things right.

Asha slipped on her sandals and hurried down the stairs. In the kitchen, Yesofu's mother, Fara, prepared lunch. She was a couple of years older than Mama and had worked for Asha's family since before Asha and her sister were born. But now with Teelu studying nursing in London and Asha being older, they didn't need an *ayah* anymore. Fara became their housegirl again—doing all the cooking and cleaning. Asha opened the front door. Weaverbirds darted out of the bougainvillea shrub, twittering as if wishing her good luck. She went to step outside when she heard footsteps approaching. Her hand tightened on the doorknob and she stopped.

"Where are you sneaking off to?" Fara asked.

Asha turned. Dried bougainvillea petals blew into the house, chasing her shadow as it stretched down the corridor toward Fara. Asha knew what was coming. Fara had a tricky way of hiding her telling-off inside a story that ended quickly but left you feeling worse as the day went on. "Um . . . I'll be right back," said Asha, but her feet refused to move. Fara's eyes trailed a path down Asha's arm, lingering on her bare wrist. She knew about the bracelet. Asha tightened her fingers around the three beads closed inside her fist.

Fara started sweeping. "Don't be long," she said. "Lunch will be ready soon."

Asha couldn't believe it. Yesofu must have told Fara what had happened, so why wasn't she angry? Swish-swish-swish. The broom moved back and forth, scooping the petals into a neat pile. Usually Fara was ready with a sermon if any of them—Asha, Yesofu, his brother, Esi, or Teelu—needed a good telling-off. Asha's shoulders sagged under the weight of Fara's silence. She stepped outside and started across the field toward the club. Yesofu's words echoed in her head. *We're different. My family works for your family.*

The sun had risen high over the rooftops and the air was getting hotter. In the distance Asha saw Simon waiting for her under the banyan tree outside the Entebbe Institute. Simon's family came from the same village in Goa as Papa and lived a couple of doors down from Asha. Last night, after Yesofu'd taken off, he'd promised he'd help look for the beads.

"What took you so long?" Simon put a piece of mango skin into his mouth and pulled off the orange flesh with his teeth before tossing it aside.

"The priest talked on and on and then Fara stopped me on my way out." Asha led him to the spot where she and Yesofu had been standing.

As the two of them searched, the sun burned hotter. Sweat trickled between Asha's shoulder blades and down her back until her thin cotton tunic stuck to her like a wet sheet. She'd been on her hands and knees, crawling through the grass, for thirty minutes.

Simon leaned against the trunk of the tree and stretched out his legs. "Tell me again why you didn't take the bracelet when he gave it to you?"

Asha had been asking herself the same question. She'd wanted the bracelet, especially when she saw the colorful beads. "He promised to come to my party and then gave that dumb excuse that he couldn't come because we're different."

"You are different."

Asha raked her fingers through the grass. She was starting to hate that word. Black. Brown. Indian. African. She'd prove Yesofu wrong. Show him these differences didn't matter. In the distance, she heard a *tum-tam-tum* bounce across the field. The back of their house faced the Entebbe Institute, so Mama banged a wooden spoon on the bottom of a metal pan when she wanted Asha or Papa to return home from the club—it was faster to knock on the pan than walk over or send a houseboy, one of the African servants.

Simon glanced at his watch. "Sorry, I have to get going. I'm meeting the guys to play field hockey." He got up and dusted off the back of his shorts.

Asha peered inside the brown paper bag. Six beads. With the three she already had, she only needed one more to put things right between her and Yesofu. "I'm going to stay and keep looking." Asha waved to Simon and got back on her hands and knees. She crawled around the long, dangling roots, prodding the dirt with her finger. At the base of the tree trunk, she saw a glimmer of orangey-gold. No rocks sparkled like that. It had to be the last one. She plucked it out of the dirt.

"Yes, ten!"

Asha rubbed the bead against her stomach, leaving long reddish-brown streaks down the front of her tunic. She held it up to the light and caught her breath. A fleck of gold shimmered inside like a tiny flame. None of the shops on India Street had beads this beautiful. Yesofu must have gone all the way to Kampala. Now she felt even worse, but at least she'd found all ten. Once she put the bracelet back together, there was no way he could stay mad at her. She was sure of it. *Tum-tam-tum.* The banging was louder with that Mamalosing-her-patience sound. Asha dropped the last bead into the bag, jumped up, and hurried home.

Sunday lunch was always followed by sweets in the sitting room. Papa pulled back the thick brocade curtains, letting in a stream of sunlight. Asha dragged out the round, leather pouf from under the coffee table. She picked up the *Uganda Argus* newspaper that lay on top. The headline stretched across the front in bold letters—PLANS FOR A NEW UGANDA. The article, written by Mr. Gupta, had a photograph of President Amin. Asha was friends with the Gupta twins—Leela and Neela. She tossed the paper aside. No time for Idi Amin. She needed to work on fixing her bracelet. Asha emptied the beads, arranging them in a straight line.

"When is Teelu coming home?" she asked Papa. Asha's sister had promised to bring a special birthday gift from London.

"I'm waiting to hear when she finishes her exams," said Papa. "Then I can arrange her visa and tickets." Asha's father worked for the ministry of tourism. He arranged special passports and visas for important dignitaries and other visiting government officials.

Papa switched on the television. Gray and white lines flickered across the screen. He twisted the antenna until the fuzziness melted together into a clear picture. President Idi Amin appeared, smiling broadly at Asha from the square television box. He looked a little like Yesofu's father, but taller and with a rounder face. The front of his uniform was covered in medals.

". . . And I promise you—as a military man I know how to act. We will build new schools, new roads, and . . ."

New schools. No thanks. Her school was just fine. New roads—yes! Especially if it meant her shoes wouldn't get covered in a thick layer of red dirt every time she went into town. Mama appeared, balancing three small bowls and two mugs of steaming *chai* on a silver tray. Her bangles softly clinked as she set the tray down on the low table. She'd recently cut her wavy hair to her shoulders and was wearing it loose instead of pulled back in a braid. Asha had the same black hair, but hers was frizzy like a lion's mane.

Mama handed a small porcelain bowl to Asha. *Kulfi!* It didn't matter how full she was, Asha always had room for ice cream.

"What is the president up to now?" Mama asked.

Papa turned up the volume and Amin's booming voice burst out of the little box like a firecracker.

". . . I stand before you wearing the uniform of a general, but don't forget I came from a very poor, poor family. I am a simple man like you . . . God spoke to me in a dream. I promise you that together you and I will make this country better and stronger and free."

Asha pressed her spoon into the soft ice cream. President Amin dreamed a lot. A couple of weeks ago he'd announced on the news that he had a dream where God spoke to him about getting rid of Indians. Good thing President Amin didn't listen to his dreams.

≈ 3 ≈
YESOFU

THE LUNCH BELL rang, and Yesofu glanced over in Asha's direction. He'd been avoiding her all morning, which wasn't easy since they were both in primary class seven together. He pretended to sort the papers on his desk until Asha left. Then he jumped up, grabbed his lunch tiffin, and headed outside.

Yesofu saw Asha laughing with Leela and Neela. Silently fuming, he gripped the handle of his lunch tiffin and walked in the opposite direction. He still couldn't believe she had broken his gift, especially when he had been saving up since his own birthday to get it. It wasn't like he had ever been to any of her parties before.

Now all he wanted to do was talk to the guys from the neighborhood—Akello, Salim, and Yasid.

13

"You should go see Coach," Salim was saying. He saw Yesofu and scooted over.

"What are you talking about?" Yesofu asked.

"Getting Akello back on the cricket team." Yasid tossed his empty banana peel into the metal bin.

Akello was thirteen—a year older than Yesofu—and also from the Ganda tribe. He and Yesofu had been the first two Africans to make the school team and dreamed of getting sports scholarships for secondary school. Or that had been their plan until a couple of months ago, when Akello'd just stopped showing up for practice. He'd told the guys that he'd been thrown off the team. But Yesofu knew that wasn't true.

"You want to come back?" he asked.

"It wouldn't matter." Akello scratched the back of his neck. "Coach only plays Indians."

Yesofu opened his mouth and shut it, as Mamma's voice whispered in his head. *Naye abasatu babisattula.* It was a Luganda saying: A secret is better kept by two than three.

"Well, Yesofu's practically Indian, but he almost never gets to pitch." Salim snickered.

"*Nyamaza!*" Yesofu cut in.

"You shut up," said Salim. "You may be a good bowler, but you hardly pitch. Coach always has Rajeev bowl."

"Come on, Yesofu is important," Yasid joined in. "He's the team benchwarmer."

14

"Leave him alone," said Akello.

Salim and Yasid walked away laughing and punching one another.

Akello reached into his pocket and pulled out two chocolates wrapped in paper. He held one out to Yesofu. "Thanks for not saying anything."

Yesofu leaned in. "I could talk to Coach about you joining us at practice—"

Akello shook his head. "I can't. . . . Not yet."

Yesofu unwrapped the chocolate. "Any word from your dad?"

"No. Guess he's still looking for work. Still, it's better than around here; the British only hire *Mhindis*."

Akello sounded like he was trying to convince himself. Yesofu kept quiet. He understood—Akello didn't want to let down or shame his family. It was the Ganda way. But Yesofu knew he'd be upset if he had to get a job instead of going to cricket practice.

"How's work?" Yesofu asked.

"*Sawa sawa*." Akello shrugged. "It's okay, but it may be changing."

"What do you mean?"

Akello put his elbows on the table and moved closer. "The guys in the sugar and coffee fields have been talking about President Amin."

"What'd they say?"

"That he has big plans. Plans to help Africans get better lives."

Yesofu had only been two when the British left Uganda, but he'd heard his brother, Esi, remembering the same sort of excitement. Baba had even tried to buy a small farm. Only the bank wouldn't sell it to an African.

"What's Idi Amin planning? How's he gonna change things?"

"More jobs. Better ones," said Akello. "Other stuff too."

Yesofu popped a piece of *chapati* in his mouth, thinking about what other stuff President Amin could change. "You mean like helping us get land . . . or a farm?"

Akello nodded. "That's not all . . . maybe even a shop, like the ones on India Street."

Yesofu pictured Mamma selling traditional African *gomesi* or *busuuti* dresses in her own shop instead of cleaning and cooking for Asha's family. She'd only finished up to primary class three, but she could measure, cut, and sew the most amazing *busuuti* dress. Mamma's eyes shined whenever she finished a new dress for herself or one of the women in the neighborhood.

"I bet if Baba could get a good job in Entebbe . . ."

Yesofu left his dreams for Mamma and listened. "What?"

"If Baba got a job, then he'd probably stick around, and then I'd be back on the team." Akello got up and pretended to hold a cricket bat in his hands.

16

"That'd be great!" Yesofu smiled. But in the back of his mind he wondered, what if Akello's father didn't come back? What if Akello couldn't pay the school fees? Asha's dad paid Yesofu's fees. But that was changing for secondary school. It was why cricket was so important.

Akello's hands dropped, and he stared past Yesofu's shoulder. "Look who's coming."

Yesofu turned. Asha was on her way over with Simon.

"*Habari*," Akello greeted them. "How was the big party?"

Yesofu elbowed Akello to make him shut up.

"Um . . . it was fun," Asha replied. She shot a quick glance at Yesofu.

He waited to see if Asha'd say anything more. She didn't. Instead, she tugged the edge of her sleeve, fidgeting with something on her wrist.

"Can we talk?" she asked Yesofu, her voice low.

"I need to go."

"We've got a few minutes," Akello said.

Yesofu scowled. He didn't need Akello's help. He shut his food tiffin and got up to leave. "You coming or what?"

"I guess we'll see you later," said Akello.

Yesofu held his lunch tiffin against his chest as he and Akello started back to class.

"Asha has a temper quick as a cobra bite," said Akello. "But she doesn't mean it."

"I can't believe you, of all people, are defending her."

17

"What? She's spoiled . . . used to getting her own way. You can't stay mad at her forever."

Yesofu glanced at Asha. She looked hurt. Her eyes were lowered, staring at her wrist. A part of him wanted to forgive her, but he couldn't forget how she'd told him he *should* have come to her party. Not asked. Ordered. Demanded.

"How long do you plan on ignoring her?" Akello asked.

Yesofu shrugged. "One more day. Then I'll talk to her."

"Wait!" Asha called out.

Behind him, Yesofu heard her hurrying. He slowed but didn't stop.

Asha caught up and held out her wrist. "Look."

Yesofu stopped. Asha had on his bracelet.

Akello's mouth dropped open. "Did you buy a new one?"

"Nope." Asha's eyes sparkled.

Yesofu stared at Asha's wrist, counting the beads. They were all there. The exact same ones he'd picked out at the shop.

She thanked him. *"Asante.* It's the best birthday present ever."

Yesofu held back a smile, but his insides puffed like the whole-wheat *puris* that Mamma cooked.

4

ASHA

"MATH QUIZ TOMORROW!" Coach shouted just as the school bell rang.

Asha hummed as she shoved her math book inside her backpack. Usually anything with numbers made her brain cringe, but nothing could ruin her good mood. She and Yesofu were talking again. She'd hoped he'd wait for her so they could walk home together, like they did every day after school, but he'd raced out when the bell rang. It didn't matter. She'd seen his face when she showed him the bracelet.

"You? Happy about a math quiz?" Neela turned to face Asha. "Either you've gone nuts or something is up."

Asha smiled and held up her arm.

"Oooh," squealed Leela and grabbed Asha's wrist. "The

beads are amazing. Who's it from?"

"I know who." Neela gave her sister a knowing look.

"Oooh," said Leela.

Asha pulled her arm out of Leela's grasp. "It's a friendship bracelet. You know Yesofu's my best friend."

"You sure about that?" Neela glanced at the window.

Outside, Yesofu stood with Akello under the banyan tree. His and Asha's meeting spot after school. Asha looked at her bracelet and then at Yesofu. Akello knew she and Yesofu were best friends. He'd even tried to help today at lunch when Yesofu was being stubborn, refusing to talk to her.

"It doesn't mean anything," Asha told Neela. "Yesofu and I have other friends."

"Quit making *matata*," Leela told her sister. "You love to make trouble."

Neela sniffed and tossed her hair back. "You'll see. I'm right." She flung her backpack over her shoulder.

Asha zipped her bag closed, hurrying so she could meet up with Yesofu. She looked out the window. Salim and Yasid had joined Akello. She searched for Yesofu. He was gone. So much for walking home together. She followed Leela and Neela outside, hating that Neela might be right.

"Can you meet Friday after school?" Leela asked.

Asha nodded. "Mama said I could go." A dance was coming up at the Entebbe Club and that meant new outfits. Teelu usually helped Asha pick out the perfect fabric for a new dress or tunic. But with her sister thousands of miles away at nursing college in London, Asha had to rely on the other fashion-obsessed person in her life—Neela. She waved bye to the twins and set off for home. Alone.

Asha usually loved the walk from school at the top of the hill to her house at the end of Lugado Street, but today it was so hot she could practically feel the heat burning through the soles of her shoes. When she turned the last corner, where she and Yesofu always started guessing what snack Fara would have waiting for them—samosas, sandwiches—Asha sighed. It wasn't as fun playing alone.

"*Jalebi! Mhogo!*" Yesofu's voice called out.

Asha looked around, but couldn't see him.

"*Chapatis*," he said, jumping out from the tree he'd been hiding behind.

Asha wished Neela was here right now so she could look her in the face and say *I told you so!*

5

YESOFU

"WHAT TOOK YOU so long?" Yesofu said. "You're so slow."

The sides of Asha's mouth twitched like she was trying hard not to smile. "Race you?" She took off before Yesofu had a chance to answer, her feet slapping as she weaved through the trees.

Yesofu raced after her. It didn't take long to catch up, and he grinned over his shoulder as he flew past. At the bottom of the hill, he leaned against a eucalyptus tree. When she'd showed him the bracelet, he'd been surprised. Shocked. He couldn't stay mad after that. Asha ran up and collapsed against him, huffing and puffing.

"When did you get so fast?" Asha said between gasps.

"I've always been fast. I just let you win sometimes."

Asha slugged him hard.

Yesofu picked up her backpack and swung it over his shoulder. "Come on."

As they continued past the houses, stacked in neat rows, Yesofu noticed how different Asha's neighborhood was from his. It wasn't like it had suddenly changed. It was more like he'd changed, noticing more and more just how different his life was compared with Asha's. Her family lived in a pale yellow two-story house. Twice . . . no, triple or quadruple the size of his place. What would Asha think of his family's tiny two-room shack if she ever came by? It definitely didn't have a huge wraparound verandah like this one.

Yesofu followed Asha up the stairs to the front door. The wooden shutters were folded open, and Yesofu could hear Mamma humming. He looked over the bougainvillea hedge into the next house. "It's so cool the twins' uncle is playing for the Ugandan field hockey team in the Olympics," he said, unable to hide the hint of envy in his voice.

"You could play in the Olympics one day," said Asha.

"They don't have cricket."

"But if you make team captain, then you could get a scholarship to secondary school and then to university and then . . ." Asha paused. "The national cricket team!"

"Maybe." Yesofu's eyes brightened and his mouth slowly spread into a toothy grin. "I'll know this week." Yesofu had a real shot at being named captain—it was between him and Rajeev. But that wasn't even the best part . . . the part he hadn't told anyone—well, except for Akello. The school team captain got to throw the first ball out at the upcoming Uganda-India cricket match. Yesofu couldn't believe it when Coach had told him. "Let's go inside."

"Not so fast." Asha grabbed his arm. "What aren't you telling me?"

"Nothing." Yesofu looked away, but Asha wasn't letting him go. "I can't. I promised Coach I wouldn't say anything."

"I knew it!" Asha danced around the verandah, hopping and waving her arms. "You've been named captain!"

"What? No."

"Then tell me," she pleaded.

"Okay." Yesofu put his hands on her shoulders to stop her bouncing. "You know the India-Uganda match?"

"Yes!" Asha rolled her eyes. "Only the biggest match of the year."

"Well, our team captain gets to pitch the first ball." Yesofu ran to the opposite side of the verandah and pitched an invisible ball to Asha.

"No way!" She jumped up and pretended to catch it. "That will so be you."

"I hope so." Yesofu ran in a circle around her. "Akello thought it was awesome too."

Asha stopped and her face clouded over.

"What's wrong?" Yesofu asked.

"You told Akello?"

"Now you both know. It's not a big deal." Yesofu pretended to throw another ball, but Asha stood with her arms still against her sides. Yesofu felt bad it bothered her that he'd told Akello first. But he did tell her. And with Akello, he really got how big a deal this could be for him.

Asha touched her bracelet. "We'll always be best friends," she said as she picked up her backpack and walked inside.

Yesofu followed, trying to figure out if she was asking him or telling.

⩨ 6 ⩨
ASHA

THAT YESOFU HAD told Akello before her had niggled at Asha all week. But she'd done her best to ignore it. It didn't mean anything, she kept telling herself whenever she saw Yesofu and Akello together. It didn't mean anything.

"Hurry up!" shouted Mr. Bhatt, the owner of Café Nile, holding the door open. *"Jaldee! Jaldee!"* As if repeating his words in Hindi made them doubly urgent. Asha, Leela, and Neela scurried in.

It was Friday and Asha had met the Gupta twins in town to shop for the upcoming dance at the Entebbe Club. Asha was on her way to the Sari House with Leela and Neela when Mr. Bhatt called them over.

"What's wrong?" Asha asked.

26

Mr. Bhatt shut the door, almost catching the end of Neela's scarf. He spun around, shaking his finger at them. "What are you doing here?"

"Shopping," said Neela. "I need a new—"

"The shops are shut." Mr. Bhatt moved them away from the door. "You shouldn't be in town. Not now. Not with all the trouble."

"What kind of trouble?" Asha and Leela asked at the same time.

Mr. Bhatt didn't answer. He waved his hand at the tables. "Go sit and don't leave!"

"Is it just me or is he acting really weird?" said Asha. Over at the counter, Mr. Bhatt kept looking in their direction as he whispered into the telephone.

"Maybe it has something to do with that."

Asha looked outside. Crowds of people poured onto India Street, in front of the long row of shops. They shouted and cheered, waving the Ugandan flag. Earlier this year, Coach Edwin had taught the class the history behind the flag—each of the three colored stripes represented a part of Africa: black for the African people, yellow for Africa's sunshine, and red for the color of blood connecting all the African people. Asha didn't have African blood, but Uganda was her home.

"It looks like some kind of parade," Neela said.

Leela squeezed between them. "Is it Independence Day?"

"That's in October," Asha replied. She craned her neck to

see farther down the street. The shops and their owners were as familiar as her neighborhood, but today she felt a strange tightness in her chest she couldn't explain. Horns beeped and men punched their fists in the air. Everybody looked happy. Jubilant. Asha glanced at Mr. Bhatt. He slammed down the phone and disappeared into the back room. Asha couldn't tell if it was the parade that had Mr. Bhatt all jumpy or if it was something else.

"Look!" Leela cried.

Outside, a group of African women in traditional *gomesi* danced past the café in a rainbow of colors. Asha loved the floor-length dresses with short, puffed sleeves and wide sash. "I should wear a *gomesi* to the club function."

"You can't," said Leela.

"Why not?"

"You'd look ridiculous," sniffed Neela.

"Don't forget, you're Indian," added Leela. "Not African."

"Indian. African. We're different, so what? If people stopped making such a big deal of it, then it wouldn't matter so much." The women had slowed down, shouting and pointing at the three of them as they passed. Asha couldn't hear what they said, but the way they were waving their arms in the air and glaring made the hairs on the back of her neck stand up. Whatever was going on in town today felt different than the usual parades and celebrations. A sudden feeling of wanting to be home overtook Asha. "I'm leaving," she announced.

Leela grabbed her arm. "But Mr. Bhatt said to—"

"I don't care," said Asha. "I'm tired of waiting."

"Me too!" Neela jumped up.

Leela glanced outside. "What about all that craziness?"

"What about it?" Asha asked. "Things will be fine once we're off India Street." She and Neela started for the door.

"Wait for me!" Leela cried. She scrambled out of her seat and squeezed between Asha and Neela, clasping their hands tightly. "Don't let go."

Asha pushed open the door and together they stepped outside. The sun beat down as Asha led the way, pushing into the crowds. The noise engulfed her like the waves of the Indian Ocean, threatening to pull her under.

"Come on." Asha tightened her grip on Leela's hand, pulling her and Neela deeper into the crowds.

7

YESOFU

"YANGUWA!" ESI SHOUTED.

Yesofu heard his brother's shouts as he and Akello came down from the well. They hurried as fast as they could, careful not to spill water from the metal pails they carried.

"Let's go," said Esi. He motioned for Yesofu and Akello to climb onto the motorbike.

Yesofu set down the water pails. He'd never seen his brother looking so frenzied. Esi was the calm one. "Always cool, that boy," Baba would say.

Today, Yesofu's brother bounced on his motorbike, waving his arms, like he was doing a Buganda tribal *nankasa* dance.

"Harakisha! Hurry up!" Esi repeated, as if the command in Luganda, Swahili, and then in English would make them

move faster. "Today's a great day for Ugandans! President Amin just made a big announcement."

"What'd he say?" Yesofu asked.

"Not now." Esi patted the back of the scooter. "Get on so we can go!"

Yesofu didn't argue. He swung his leg over the seat and scooted forward to make room for Akello.

"Where to?" Akello asked. He climbed on behind Yesofu.

"India Street . . ." Esi's voice disappeared, swallowed by the grinding motorbike engine.

Yesofu held on tightly as his brother maneuvered up and down the small hills leading into the main part of Entebbe . . . away from the rural area where they lived. Yesofu flung his arm around his brother's waist as the bike hit another rut and bounded into the air. He felt Akello grab him from behind. Whatever was happening must be really good for Esi to be driving this fast. As they neared India Street, Esi slowed. People, *boda-boda* taxis, cars, and cyclists spilled onto the street.

"Hold on." Esi swerved into a narrow alleyway leading to the center of India Street and parked the bike behind two empty oil drums. They climbed off and continued by foot.

Yesofu grabbed Akello's arm and pointed. Up ahead, a wall of people stretched from one end of India Street to the other. Some marched down the middle of the street. Others stood on crates and tables. Groups peered down from rooftops. Yesofu felt dizzy staring down at the crowds. Independence

Day parades had tons of people, but not this much excitement. Whatever it was that President Amin had announced had to be something really big.

"Esi, up here!" someone called out.

Yesofu looked up. It was one of his brother's friends.

Esi turned over an empty oil barrel and used it to climb onto the roof of the Sari House. "Give me your hands," he said, and pulled Yesofu and Akello up.

They made their way to the edge of the building, pushing past the group that had gathered. Looking out from the rooftop, Yesofu had a clear view of India Street. There were people everywhere, waving the Ugandan flag, cheering and chanting. It was the biggest crowd he'd ever seen. An African man jumped over from the next-door building.

"Good day for Africans." The man handed Yesofu and Akello Ugandan flags. "President Amin ordered Indians to go home—to leave Uganda." The man clapped his hand against his chest. "Finally, Africans will get what they deserve. Opportunities are there *for us*." The man hollered and walked away.

Akello hopped back and forth, waving his flag. "Go Dada Amin."

The man's words turned inside Yesofu. It wasn't just the opportunities opening up for Africans but also the bit about Indians being kicked out. Did that mean all Indians—Asha too?

"It's happening." Akello nudged Yesofu. "Our lives are gonna change."

Yesofu looked at the flag in his hand. The Ugandan flag—six bands of black, yellow, and red repeated twice with a grey crowned crane perched in the center inside a white circle. The red band was for the blood of the African people. It connected them. *Africans will finally get what they deserve.* Yesofu looked out at the growing excitement.

"Did you hear me?" Akello shouted over the cheers. "We're gonna live in real houses with walls and running water."

"No more carrying water from the well," Yesofu added.

Akello grabbed Yesofu's shoulders. "No more working the sugar and coffee fields." They jumped in circles, and Yesofu's worries about Asha faded.

For as long as he could remember, Yesofu'd wanted more than to go out into the fields every day like Baba. Or to cook and clean for *mzungu* or Indians like Mamma. There wasn't anything wrong with it, but compared to finishing college or playing professional cricket? It wasn't even a contest. He wanted to be able to buy Baba a real house, maybe even get Mamma her own housegirl.

What had that man said?

Africans will finally get what they deserve.

Yesofu repeated the words, breathing life into them, fighting to ignore every what-if. What if he didn't get a cricket scholarship? What if they couldn't afford the fees at Entebbe Secondary School?

Africans will finally get what they deserve.

Now Yesofu cheered and waved his Ugandan flag. President Amin was going to help. A change was coming.

≋ 8 ≋

ASHA

ASHA TIGHTENED HER grip on Leela's hand. The crowds spread across India Street, making it almost impossible to cross. People huddled together in groups, waving the Ugandan flag, or danced with their arms linked together. The three of them had hardly moved at all, being pushed and pulled back and forth. The heat of the sun and the people made it hard to breathe, or maybe it was the fear of being trapped and unable to get out. Why hadn't she listened to Mr. Bhatt and stayed inside Café Nile? It was too late now.

"*Mhindi . . .*"

Indian. The word thundered all around. Asha's chest tightened as she looked for spaces to push through, past the jutting elbows and dancing bodies. She looked up at the dark faces shining with excitement and felt none of their joy.

"Dada Amin!"

The crowd cheered for the president, their chanting growing louder and louder. A thick mass of bodies moved in. Asha squeezed Leela's hand and she squeezed back.

"Wahindi waende nyumbani!"

Indians go home. That's what she was trying to do. Suddenly, a wave of people pitched forward, tugging, to pull them apart. Asha felt Leela's fingers tighten. A heavy mass slammed against Asha. She hit the ground. Leela's hand was gone.

Asha had to get up before she got trampled. She rolled onto her knees and stood. Where were Leela and Neela? She spun around, searching through the unfamiliar faces coming upon her. She felt a hand wrap around her wrist. Dark fingers. Not Leela or Neela. Asha yanked to get free, but the fingers tightened. She felt herself being pulled with a grip that was almost painful. Her heart hammered against her chest and her breath came out in gasps. The person holding on to her moved quickly until finally they escaped the crowds and stopped.

Asha looked up. Esi! He'd found her like that time she got separated from him and Yesofu after seeing Independence Day fireworks at Lake Victoria. She threw her arms around his neck. "I'm so glad it's you."

"What are you doing here?"

Asha jumped back, shocked by the anger in his voice. Esi

had that same look on his face as Mr. Bhatt—a crisscross of worry.

"*Wahindi waende nyumbani!*" The shouts thundered around them.

"Why are they shouting 'Indians go home'?"

"I'm getting you out of here," said Esi.

Asha stepped back as Esi reached for her. She wasn't going anywhere. "Not until you tell me what's going on!"

"Later. We just have to go. Right now."

A police car appeared, its siren blaring. A flash of fear swept across Esi's face. He lunged toward her, but Asha stepped out of his reach.

"You almost got trampled," snapped Esi. He pointed up. "What would have happened if Yesofu hadn't seen you?"

Yesofu was here? Asha looked to where Esi pointed. Yesofu and Akello stood on top of Sari House, bouncing from foot to foot, cheering, waving, and hollering. A different kind of fear gripped Asha. The kind that left her wondering what her best friend was doing on top of the Sari House with a huge smile on his face while everyone around him shouted for Indians to leave. She looked down at the friendship bracelet on her wrist. There had to be a good reason Yesofu was here. She made a move toward him when Esi grabbed her hand, pulling her in the opposite direction.

"*Wahindi waende nyumbani!*"

Esi kept a quick, steady pace. He dragged her away from

India Street into an alley, finally letting go when he reached his scooter. "Get on."

Asha climbed up, settling behind Esi. She wrapped her arms around him, holding on tightly as he started weaving through the crowds. When they got closer to Asha's house, Esi slowed, finally coming to a stop at the top of her street.

"You can get home from here," Esi told her.

Asha climbed off. Esi was the older brother she and Teelu never had. But something felt different today. "Why won't you tell me what's going on?"

Esi rubbed the back of his neck. Finally he looked at her. "Asha, things are going to be changing . . ." He paused like he wasn't sure if he should continue. "The president made an announcement."

"What?"

"He wants Indians to leave. He wants them out of Uganda."

"You're lying."

Esi shook his head.

"You need to go home, Asha. Talk to your parents."

Asha didn't wait. She took off running, willing her legs to move faster. Uganda was home. The president couldn't *make* her leave. Her heart thumped in step with her feet. As she skidded through the open gate, she saw Papa's car. Asha leapt up the verandah and ran inside the house.

"Papa!" Asha cried out.

Both Mama and Papa came running out of the sitting room. Papa opened his arms and Asha ran into them. He pulled her close, holding her like he used to when she'd fall and scrape her knee.

"Is it true?" Asha asked, stopping to catch her breath. "Is the president kicking us out?"

"Yes."

Papa's words were barely a whisper, but they felt like a burst of thunder crashing on top of her head.

90 DAYS

9

YESOFU

THE EXCITEMENT OF yesterday was still with Yesofu as he finished his morning chores. He snapped the longer branches and added them to the pile of firewood by his home made of wattle and daub—woven rods and twigs plastered with clay and mud. Inside, the hut was quiet under the grass roof. Mamma and Baba woke with the early sun. Mamma caught the bus to Asha's house and Baba joined other men from the village to work in the fields. Yesofu glanced at the mat across from him. It was empty. Esi had left to drive Asha's father to work. Would that change soon?

The president was returning Uganda to Africans.

Wahindi waende nyumbani. That's what everyone had been chanting yesterday. What he had been chanting. Yesofu hadn't been able to get Asha out of his head after he and Akello had seen her yesterday. She'd looked like a trapped animal in the crowd of Africans. Esi had assured him she was fine, but Yesofu'd been wondering what the expulsion meant for Asha. Baba had said that Mr. Gomez had Ugandan citizenship, which meant Asha didn't have to go.

Yesofu finished the last bite of his porridge and set the bowl inside the bucket of water. His thoughts kept spinning back to Asha. She was Indian. So were his friends on the cricket team—Simon and Rajeev. What would happen to the cricket team if their parents didn't have Ugandan citizenship?

Yesofu pulled on his uniform—tan shorts and a buttoned white, short-sleeved shirt. His white socks were a reddish tan from the dust, so he turned them inside out and found his shoes. He grabbed his backpack and set off for school.

Walking the narrow, unpaved road leading into town, Yesofu passed women balancing baskets of fruit and vegetables on their heads. He waved at Akello's mamma and sisters. Men in groups waited for the bus. Conversation fluttered around Yesofu like the yellow weavers darting in and out of the elephant grass.

"No more cleaning and cooking for those Indians."

"My children will see a new Uganda . . . Amin will make sure of that."

"A Uganda for Africans . . . not *Wahindi* or *mzungu*."

44

Yesofu noticed the person spat out the words for Indians and whites like they were poison on his tongue. A slight shiver ran up his spine.

Salim and Yasid ran up, appearing on either side of Yesofu.

"*Hujambo*," said Yesofu.

"Day one," said Yasid. "Start packing, Indians."

Salim looked at Yesofu. "You too."

"I'm not going anywhere."

"Oh, right," said Salim. "You're African. I keep forgetting." He and Yasid snickered. "What about your girlfriend?"

Running feet approached from behind, and Akello joined them. "What's up?"

"We were asking about Asha."

Yesofu faced Salim. "What about her?"

"What does she think of Dada Amin's plan?" Yasid asked.

Akello shot them a look that said *Back off!* But neither seemed to notice.

"You always say she's different from other Indians—" Salim put on a smile, so big and fake that Yesofu wanted to smack it off his face.

"Asha will get what this means to me . . . to us."

"You're crazy," said Salim, laughing as he and Yasid ran ahead.

Yesofu stood up straight. They didn't know Asha like he did. She'd know how the president's plan could help him and

45

other Africans. He turned to Akello.

"Asha will understand." He meant to sound sure, but it came out more like a question.

Akello looked at him and shrugged. "I like Asha . . . she's okay, but I'm not sure she'll understand."

≋ 10 ≋

ASHA

WALKING INTO COACH'S class, Asha couldn't get the memory of Yesofu cheering out of her head. She clasped her friendship bracelet, pressing the beads into her wrist. Yesofu had Indian friends other than her. Did he really want them kicked out? Did Indians have to leave so Africans could have a better life?

Asha crinkled her nose against the early morning blast of lemon disinfectant and looked around the classroom. Like oil and water, Indians and Africans shared the space without mixing. It wasn't any different than usual, but somehow President Amin's announcement made it feel entirely different.

"Over here," Leela called.

Asha squeezed past a group, including Salim and Yasid.

Usually Yesofu and Akello hung out with them, but she didn't see either of them.

"Doing okay after yesterday?" Leela asked.

Before Asha could answer, Neela jumped in. "It's so awful." She threw her head down on her desk. Usually Neela was over the top about everything, but today was the first time that Asha felt like doing the same thing.

"Your dad writes for the *Uganda Argus*," said Asha. "You'll be fine."

"We have British passports," said Leela. "If the president gets his way, he'll kick us out."

Asha didn't want to think about the twins leaving. She shook her head. "That won't happen. President Amin is crazy."

Salim appeared at Asha's side. "Who are you calling crazy?" He grabbed her backpack.

Asha glared at him and he glared back. She lunged for her bag.

"I asked you a question."

"So what?" Asha shot back. "I don't have to answer."

"If you want this . . ." Salim shook her bag in the air. "You do."

Other kids started crowding in. Leela and Neela stood on either side of Asha.

"She called President Amin crazy . . . because he is." Neela stood with her hands on her hips and her chin jutting out.

Shouts erupted from the African kids. Asha elbowed Neela and shot her a look that told her to keep her big mouth shut.

"Come on . . . what President Amin is doing is wrong," Asha said.

"For whom?" Akello walked up to her. Right behind, Yesofu followed. He snatched the backpack out of Salim's hand and returned it to Asha.

"*Asante*," she thanked him. They'd always talked in this mix of Swahili and English. He'd tried to teach her his tribal language, Luganda, but she still only knew a couple of words.

"Who's it wrong for?" Yesofu asked.

"Us . . . it's wrong for us." Asha searched his face for a sign that he understood how awful it was for President Amin to make Indians leave their home . . . their country.

"You mean it's wrong for Indians," Yesofu shot back. "Because from where I'm standing, everything he's doing is *right*."

Asha couldn't believe it. Yesofu was supposed to be her best friend. How could he think what the president was doing was okay?

Akello stepped forward. "President Amin is helping Africans get what they deserve. This is our country. The *mzungu*—whites—got rich off us, and when the British left, the Indians stepped right in taking . . . taking. Now it's our turn!"

Asha stared at Yesofu, waiting for him to disagree with

Akello, but he just stood there nodding. "You believe that?" Asha twisted her bracelet around her wrist, anger rising in her. "Indians make less money doing exactly the same jobs as the British."

"But we make even less than Indians," Yesofu shot back, faster than Asha expected. "Don't Esi and Mamma deserve more than being *your* slaves—don't I?"

The class grew quiet. The fire in Yesofu's eyes had disappeared, replaced with something else—disappointment.

"I told you," said Akello. He threw his arm around Yesofu's shoulder, and Yesofu didn't make any move to get away. "It's okay, though, you have us."

Why was Akello making things harder? They weren't friends like her and Yesofu. But they still got along. Or used to. Every muscle in Asha's body tensed. She waited for Yesofu to say something, counting the seconds, which were starting to feel like minutes. Finally, he shrugged like he was done talking and went off with Akello.

"Don't worry about him," Leela whispered. "He'll come around."

Asha swallowed the lump in her throat. On the night of her birthday, Yesofu'd told her they were different, making it a big deal, like she didn't know she was Indian and he was African. She knew they weren't the same. They lived in different parts of town. Fara and Esi worked for Mama and Papa. It had been like this ever since she could remember.

The door opened and Coach Edwin walked in. His eyes moved across the room, taking in the chaos. "Everyone, back to your regular seats. Now!"

Asha held her breath, knowing any second Yesofu would show up in his usual seat next to her. Finally, he came over and sat down. She leaned closer. "Yesofu—" Suddenly her throat went dry.

Yesofu crossed his arms and sat with his back tall and straight.

Asha couldn't lose this chance to let him know that she did understand. "I know we are different, but it doesn't matter."

Yesofu kept his eyes down. "It does . . ."

"Only if you let it."

Asha waited. Yesofu didn't answer.

≋ 11 ≋
YESOFU

YESOFU COULDN'T WAIT to get to cricket practice. He needed to wind up his arms, feel the power in his legs, and run until Asha and everything that happened today faded into the background.

The first sound Yesofu heard as he came up on the field was a loud *thwack*—the cricket bat smacking the ball. Rajeev stood on the batting crease line near the wicket, then swung, sending another ball flying over the head of the bowler out into the field. Yesofu needed to get out there and show Coach his skills if he wanted to be named team captain instead of Rajeev.

"No need to suit up," Coach called out to Yesofu. "I've got an announcement."

"No Africans on the team," someone called out.

"We're kicking you out!" another player shouted.

Behind him, Yesofu heard snickering. His face got hot. With Akello gone, he was the only African player on the team. Cricket was the one place he thought things would stay the same. Teammates. Didn't that count for something?

"Ignore them," said Simon. He dropped next to Yesofu and pulled out his leg guards. "They're jerks." When Yesofu first joined the cricket team, the other players had purposely hit him with the ball until Simon stood up for him. Today it felt like those first days all over again. At least he still had Simon on his side.

"Are you sure you should be hanging out with me?" Yesofu asked.

Simon tightened the straps around his leg. "You're not the one making us leave. Idi Amin is. And here—" He pointed to the cricket field. "We're on the same team."

Yesofu pulled Simon up and they joined the rest of the team. Coach Edwin blew his whistle and waited for everyone to quiet down.

"Our school was chosen to throw the ball in the Uganda-India cricket match this year."

Everyone cheered.

"Isn't it great?" Yesofu high-fived Simon. "Coach told me and Rajeev the other day and I've been waiting for you to find out."

Coach continued. "And the person throwing to the bowler will be our team captain."

This was what Yesofu had been waiting for. All the extra hours practicing were finally going to pay off. He was going to be on the field with real players from the Ugandan national team. Maybe he'd even get to meet his hero, Sam Walusimbi. It didn't matter that he wasn't playing in the official match. Just throwing the first ball to the bowler and being able to sit on the bench with the players from the national team would feel like he was a part of the team. Last night, for extra luck, Yesofu'd prayed to God and put a coffee bean in the basket as a small offering to his Ganda ancestors. By doing both, he figured he stood a better chance. *Let it be me.*

"It wasn't an easy decision," said Coach. "Only two players are skilled at both batting and bowling—Rajeev and Yesofu. Our two all-rounders."

Simon elbowed Yesofu and he nudged him right back.

"And our new captain is—" Coach paused. "Rajeev."

Every muscle in Yesofu's body tensed. Coach had always treated him the same as any of the other guys on the team. But today, Yesofu wondered if picking Rajeev was a way to stick it to President Amin. Rajeev stood next to Coach, his shoulders slumped. If that was Yesofu, he'd have been whooping and hollering. Most of the other players rushed forward, crowding around Rajeev. Yesofu hung back. Rajeev leaned close to Coach and whispered to him.

Coach raised his hand to quiet everyone.

"Thanks, Coach," said Rajeev. "But I can't—"

Yesofu looked at Simon and mouthed, "What's going on?"

Coach put his arm around Rajeev's shoulders. "Rajeev's family is leaving Entebbe."

Everyone turned to look at Yesofu, like he was the one making Rajeev leave. He looked down, avoiding their glares.

"Quiet!" Coach shouted. "It's only fair that Rajeev gets to pick his replacement."

Yesofu gripped the cricket ball in his hand. "It's over."

"You don't know that," said Simon.

"Rajeev is leaving because Idi Amin is kicking Indians out. There's no way he'll name me. Anyway, I don't know if I want it anymore. Not like this . . . because Rajeev *had* to leave." Yesofu kicked at the dirt.

"There's only one person I can think of to replace me," said Rajeev. "And Coach agrees." He paused. "Yesofu!"

Blood rushed to Yesofu's head and pounded in his ears. Rajeev had named him. But it didn't feel like a win. Nobody said a word. No cheers or claps on the back like they'd done for Rajeev.

"Ignore them," said Simon. "You deserve it. Rajeev picked you."

Yesofu straightened his shoulders and looked at Coach. "I don't want it."

Rajeev walked over to Yesofu and faced the team. "Yesofu

is the best player here . . . after me." He handed Yesofu the ball.

Coach looked at Yesofu. "Well?"

Yesofu looked at the ball in his hands. Of all the times he'd dreamed of this moment, he never thought it would feel this messy, this strange. Yesofu thought about the makeshift cricket field he, Akello, and Yasid had made. They'd picked out the flattest area they could find—near the water well, away from where a stray ball could knock out a roof. It had no green grass, and two worn mats marked the crease and the pitcher's mound. He looked around at his teammates. They had always practiced on a real cricket field.

Yesofu stood taller. "I'm in."

"We have a new captain," said Coach. "And remember, on the cricket field, we're a team. Nothing else matters."

Yesofu looked at Rajeev. He had imagined becoming team captain for so long. But now that he had it, the win felt less like a victory.

75 DAYS

≋ 12 ≋

ASHA

ASHA THREW ON her dressing gown and snatched the carrom striker off her night table before heading downstairs
to breakfast. She slipped her hand into her pocket, rolling
the striker between her fingers, hoping there'd be time to
play a game with Papa. For the past two weeks, he'd gone
straight from work to the Entebbe Institute, staying late into
the night to discuss President Amin's announcement with
friends, including the twins' dad, Mr. Gupta, and Simon's
dad.

Yesterday, the president changed his mind and exempted
a whole group of Indians from having to leave—civil servant employees and medical professionals—but the rest still
had to go. Asha knew that Papa had been worried about

Mama since she had British citizenship, but Mama was a midwife at the Grade A hospital. Now both her parents were exempt.

The Gomez family wasn't going anywhere.

The family gathered for breakfast in the kitchen. Fara stood at the counter, kneading and rolling *chapati* dough into six-inch circles, while Mama fried the dough in the *tava*. The *chapati* sizzled in the flat pan. Papa was on the phone with Teelu, getting dates so he could book her ticket home. Asha pushed in her sister's empty chair, wishing she was already here. Asha walked over to where Mama stood with Fara at the cooker. She wrapped her arms around Mama's waist, squeezing a morning greeting while breathing the warm doughy smell of cooking *chapatis*. For the first time in the last couple of weeks, things felt normal. Like they used to before President Amin decided Indians should leave.

"*Habari malaika.*" Fara used Asha's nickname—angel.

Asha smiled and rested her chin on Fara's shoulder, reaching around her to poke the *chapati* dough. She jumped back when Fara playfully smacked her hand.

"Day fifteen," the announcer boomed from Mama's radio transistor.

Every day the radios and newspapers broadcasted the number counting up to the ninety-day deadline. Asha hated how the number stayed with her, popping up in the middle of a math lesson or when playing carrom at the club. As she set the plates on the table, she thought about President Amin and how he'd changed his mind by exempting some people. If only he'd changed it to get rid of the countdown for good.

Then things could really go back to the way they used to be.

"Seventy-five days remaining for Indians to get out," the announcer declared.

"Shut that thing off." Papa hung up the phone and picked up a *chapati*.

Mama stiffened, but didn't turn around from the cooker. Fara dusted the floury *chapati atta* from her hands and switched off the radio. Mama slipped a *chapati* onto Asha's plate and pressed the spatula against the puffed dome. A soft whistling escaped. Papa spread a thick layer of guava jam on his *chapati* with concentration. Asha knew that look—it was the one he got when he had something to say that he knew Mama wouldn't like. He'd looked exactly the same the day the new British guy at the tourism office got a promotion, even though Papa had worked at the job longer and knew more.

Asha bit off a piece of *chapati* and waited.

"We may need to look at getting out now, before things become worse," said Papa.

Asha's head snapped up. "Why should we leave? Entebbe is our home."

Mama turned from the cooker. She wiped her forehead with the back of her hand, leaving whitish-brown floury streaks of *chapati atta*. "Things will settle down."

Papa pushed his plate away, leaving his *chapati* half eaten. "And what if they don't? Look how many people have left already."

"It's only because they have to," said Mama. "We're exempted."

Asha sat up straight, nodding in agreement with Mama. "Why go if we don't have to?"

"You can't pretend that President Amin doesn't want us out."

"He's not making us leave." Mama paused. "You are."

"And don't forget," Asha added, feeling more certain, "Mama delivered one of President Amin's babies when he was a general in the army. That has to count for something. Right?"

Papa ignored Asha and continued. "So it's okay for Amin to kick certain Indians out, while you stay?"

"Ashok!" Mama's face flushed and her hand trembled as she shook the *tava* at Papa. Fara came over and removed the hot pan from Mama's hands.

"What Amin's doing isn't right," said Papa, his voice steady and strong. He leaned back and folded his arms across his chest. "England is taking in Indians with British passports. How long do you think that is going to last? I'm telling you it won't be long before they say no, and then what will we do?"

"Nothing," said Asha. "We'll be in Entebbe. Who cares what England does?"

"We are fine here," Mama said, fiddling with the gold bangles on her wrist. The set of twelve thin bangles had been a present from Papa on their wedding day. She looked Papa right in the eyes. "I'm not leaving."

Asha looked back and forth between her parents. Entebbe was as much their home as it was the home of the Africans Idi Amin wanted to help. Mama understood that. Why didn't Papa? Mama's bangles clinked softly as she slid them down her arm.

"I'm not leaving, Ashok," Mama said again, quieter, but still firm.

Papa got up and wrapped his arms around her shoulders. "Okay," he sighed. "I'll take my papers to the immigration office in Kampala today."

All the ugliness between them melted away like the *ghee* in the hot *tava* as Mama rested her head on Papa's shoulder. "Thank you."

Mama had won . . . this time. But Asha had a feeling Papa wasn't done. He had that look on his face—determined and unwavering. Asha took a bite of her *chapati*, chewing with the same determination.

Uganda was her home . . . their home.

Asha glanced at Papa. He'd agreed with Mama too quickly. Somehow she had to make sure he didn't change his mind.

☀ 13 ☀
YESOFU

"SO HOW MUCH have you got?" Akello asked Yesofu on their way to work in the fields.

"Twenty shillings. A couple more Saturdays and I should have enough." Baba had made it clear that if Yesofu wanted a new cricket uniform for the Uganda-India match, he'd have to buy it himself. The truck driving Yesofu, Baba, Akello, and the other workers to the plantations slowed and turned, its engine clanking.

"Why do you need a new one?" Baba asked. "There's a perfectly good one at home."

By perfectly good, Baba meant the secondhand uniform with threadbare knees and patches of grass stains. "I can't wear that."

Good thing the bigger plantations were hiring extra workers to help cut and gather the sugarcanes. The upcoming match was a big deal, and Yesofu wanted a new uniform so he fit in with the players from the national team.

"This cricket is a waste," said Baba. "Working in the fields is fair, honest work."

Yesofu stared at the fields—a mishmash of green, gold, and brown. "I want more. I don't want to be stuck, trapped inside a jail of canes." The minute the words were out of his mouth, he wished he could have sucked them back in. The slap on the back of his head came swift and quick.

"That coach is putting crazy ideas into your head," said Baba.

Yesofu knew his father used to be just as good at cricket as he was. Probably even better. But there was no Ugandan team back then. The only way the British let an African on the cricket field was if they were carrying a tray of food or drinks. There was no changing Baba's mind. The truck stopped and everyone jumped off. The sun was hot against the back of Yesofu's neck and he pulled up the collar of his shirt, ready to get to work. He and Akello followed a few feet behind Baba.

"Do you think Sam Walusimbi's gonna be there?" Akello rolled down the sleeves of his shirt to protect his arms from getting scratched by the dried canes.

"You bet he will." Yesofu had been going over what he'd say to his hero. He didn't want to sound cheesy. It had to be something cool.

"You're so lucky."

"I know," Yesofu said to Akello, joking. "Don't worry. I'll introduce you."

"What if President Amin shows up?" Akello handed Yesofu rolls of twine.

"You think he would?"

Akello shrugged. "You never know. He's been staying at the State House more."

Baba picked up a machete and called to them. Yesofu and Akello hurried to catch up. In the fields, men stood in cutting lines, swinging at the stalks. Baba joined them. For the next four hours, Yesofu worked alongside Akello. They followed behind Baba, gathering the chopped stalks into piles, tying them with twine, and hauling them onto carts. The tall canes cut off any breeze, making it blistering hot. Yesofu couldn't imagine Rajeev or Simon having to work this hard for a new cricket uniform. When the break whistle finally blew, Yesofu's mouth was as dry as sawdust.

Out in the open, he could finally breathe. Yesofu whipped off his long-sleeved shirt and lifted his arms up. The breeze felt good.

"Hey," said Akello. "You're killing me with your stink."

Yesofu grabbed Akello's head and shoved it into his armpit. He pushed him away and they raced to where the men stood by the water well. "Do you really think that all Indians have to go for us to get what we deserve?" Yesofu asked after gulping down an entire cup of water.

"It's what Dada Amin believes, and so do I. An Africa for Africans."

Yesofu wanted to believe that President Amin could give him the life he deserved, but he couldn't forget his friends. "What about Asha and Simon?"

"What about them?" Akello faced Yesofu.

"They've lived here just as long as we have—"

"In their big houses with fancy cars." Akello cut him off. "It's not like they hang out with us, except at school. They can still have the good life, but go do it somewhere else. India. London." He looked at Yesofu with a steady seriousness in his eyes. "You should know that."

"Why me?"

"You're team captain." Akello's eyes narrowed. "Because Rajeev left?"

Yesofu bit down hard on a piece of sugarcane, his anger simmering. He didn't need Akello rubbing it in about him only getting captain because of Rajeev leaving. Yesofu had been feeling sick about it, but it wasn't like he could bring

Rajeev back. He was team captain now. The break whistle blew.

"You coming?" Akello asked.

Yesofu got up. The heat felt suffocating. Or maybe it was that deep down he knew Akello was right.

≈ 14 ≈

ASHA

ASHA CLUTCHED THE bag tightly as she ran to meet Simon at the Botanical Gardens. She saw him talking with his cousins under a eucalyptus tree and waved, hurrying over.

"Do you have it?" Simon asked.

Asha handed him the bag. When Simon told her that Yesofu'd been named team captain, she knew he'd want something special to wear. "Yesofu is going to freak out when he sees what we got him." Rajeev's uniform was the perfect surprise. She only hoped that he wouldn't also freak out when he saw her. The last time they'd talked was at school the day after President Amin's announcement.

Simon glanced at his watch. "Come on, we better go."

Situated on the northern shores of Lake Victoria, the

gardens were one of Asha's favorite places. She always imagined it was a magical forest as she walked past the exotic trees, thick flowering branches, and monkeys hiding in the dense foliage. Asha looked for Yesofu under the ancient banyan tree with its circle of hanging roots. "I don't see him."

"Wait here." Simon pointed to a patch of grass. "I'll look on the other side."

Asha had hardly stretched out her legs when she saw Yesofu. But when she sat up to wave, her mouth went dry. Akello! She didn't get why Yesofu was still hanging out with him. *Remember why you're here*, Asha said to herself. She waved and called out. "*Habari!*"

"Hi." Yesofu sat down and leaned back against a hanging tree root.

Akello dropped down next to Asha. "What are you doing here?"

Asha swallowed her irritation and scooted over. She wasn't going to let Akello get to her. Not today. Simon ran up and joined them.

"*Habari*," Yesofu greeted him. "What's that?" He pointed to a package in Simon's hand.

Simon smiled and handed Asha the bag. She whipped it open. "Surprise!"

Yesofu leaned forward and looked inside. Asha held her breath and waited. Yesofu wasn't saying anything. He didn't look happy. He looked confused, like he didn't quite know what he was looking at. "It's a cricket uniform."

"I see that," said Yesofu. "Why are you giving it to me?"

"For the Uganda-India match." Asha shook the bag, trying to hide her irritation. "Here, take it."

Yesofu made no move to take the bag. "You bought me a uniform?"

"Well, no." Asha looked to Simon for help.

"It was Rajeev's," said Simon.

For a minute, Yesofu said nothing. Then he spoke slowly, his voice almost quivering. "I don't want his hand-me-downs."

Asha stared at Yesofu. She didn't understand why he wasn't excited. His uniform was falling apart. She leaned forward. "Yesofu." He tugged a blade of grass, avoiding her gaze. Oh. How could she have been so stupid? This game was a big deal to Yesofu. Big enough that for once he wanted . . . no, he deserved a new uniform. "Yesofu," she tried again.

Akello slapped the bag out of Asha's hand. "He doesn't want Rajeev's stinky uniform."

Asha picked up the bag, wanting to whop Akello on the head with it. Instead, she ignored him and gathered all her anger into her fingers, folding up the bag tightly. "I'm sorry for making you feel like . . ."

"Like a servant that needs his rich Indian friends to buy his clothes." Akello spat out the word *Indian* as if it tasted bitter in his mouth.

"Shut up!" Asha shouted. She was sick of Akello butting in

where he didn't belong.

"You'd make things a lot better if you listened to Dada Amin and left."

Asha faced Akello. "We don't have to. Mama is exempted and Papa has Ugandan citizenship." She gripped the bag tightly, trying to keep her voice from shaking.

"Don't be so sure," said Akello. "I hear the government is revoking Indian citizenships."

Yesofu's head jerked in her direction even though she hadn't said a word.

"They can't just take away our citizenship," said Simon.

"Yes they can." Akello crossed his arms and leaned back against the tree trunk, looking triumphant. "This is *our* country. You don't belong here."

Revoked. An uneasy feeling began to settle in the pit of Asha's stomach. Papa had gone to Kampala to verify his citizenship. She shoved the bag at Simon. "I've got to go."

"Wait!" Simon called. "I'll come with you."

Asha ignored him and took off.

≋ 15 ≋
YESOFU

YESOFU SAT ON the step outside his house and pulled out the money he'd been saving. No hand-me-down cricket uniform for him. It was bad enough he was only captain because Rajeev had left. There was no way he was going to wear Rajeev's uniform too. It's not that he wanted Asha to buy him a new one, but she didn't even ask. She just expected him to be grateful. He didn't mind wearing used uniforms at school, but this was the Uganda-India cricket match. Asha should have known better. Even now his face got hot just thinking about it. Wait until they saw him in his new uniform. He held out his hand. "You sure I have enough?" he asked Esi.

His brother nodded. "The Indian *duka* owners are selling their businesses before they leave. Barter. You'll get it for less." Esi dropped some coins into Yesofu's hand. "Here's a little extra. Go grab a snack at Café Nile with Akello too."

"*Asante.*"

Outside, the morning sounds of the village were alive. The steady thumping, *thad-da, thad-da,* of dried beans being ground under heavy, wooden pestles. Mamma stood by the side of their hut, sweeping. Her neat rows of braids danced on her head as she swished the broom back and forth. She stopped when she spotted Yesofu, and he went over.

"I am very proud of you, *mwanangu.*" She pulled him into a hug that smelled of smoky firewood and onions.

"I just wish Baba wouldn't give me such a hard time about playing cricket. That's how I'll get a scholarship to pay for secondary school." Yesofu shook his head.

Mamma rested her chin on top of the broom handle. "He wants a better life for you and Esi. He does. But it's hard for him. He doesn't want you to be disappointed . . . like he was."

"I have to try." Yesofu kissed Mamma.

"He won't say it, but he's proud of you too," said Mamma. She slipped her hand into her pocket and pulled out some coins. "You and Akello be careful. Soldiers are crawling in town like ants upon a kernel of corn."

Akello wasn't outside when Yesofu went to meet him. He was about to call out when he heard shouts coming from inside the hut.

"You listen here," a male voice bellowed. It had to be

Akello's dad. That meant Akello could join the cricket team again. "You won't be needing any school clothes, 'cause you aren't going back."

What? Yesofu froze. He stood still, trying to make sense of what he was hearing. Akello had to quit the cricket team the last time his dad left. If he quit school, he'd never get into secondary school. No secondary school meant no college. And if anyone could make it to Makerere University, it would be Akello. School stuff came easy to him. Yesofu had to read and reread the text to make the information stick.

"I can't quit school," Yesofu heard Akello say. He fist-pumped the air. The father's word was respected in the Buganda tribe, but this was too important for Akello not to argue.

"How else am I going to get into Makerere?"

"College?" Akello's dad scoffed. "How you gonna pay for that? It ain't free."

"I'll get a scholarship. My grades are good and—"

"You've got more school than I got," Akello's dad cut him off. "You don't need no more."

Yesofu didn't feel like he should be listening.

"I'm not leaving school."

"Well, I'm not wasting another shilling on school fees. You aren't going back!"

Akello flew outside, almost crashing into Yesofu. "What are you looking at?"

"Nothing," Yesofu said quickly, not wanting Akello to know that he'd heard everything.

"Well, let's go." Akello set off. "We've got a uniform to buy."

For the next thirty minutes, they walked side by side in awkward silence. Bicycles, cars, and carts pulled by cattle passed, lifting red dirt onto them.

50 DAYS

≋ 16 ≋
ASHA

ASHA STARED AT the crowds spilling into the park. Papa had got them seats behind the wicketkeeper so they would be right on top of the action, but today they set up their chairs and mats on the grassy slope. Asha preferred sitting here. It's where she and Teelu always sat. Asha rolled out her woven mat and settled down. It was the perfect view to see Yesofu when he threw the first pitch to the bowler. And she was going to be the one cheering the loudest. She'd even worn her bright orange tunic to stand out. Asha kicked off her sandals and lay back. Behind her, she could hear Coach, his parents, Mr. and Mrs. Patel, and Papa and Mama talking in hushed voices as they unpacked the food. Their words floated past Asha in bits and pieces.

"Worried."

"For now."

"Move him soon."

The hair on the back of her neck prickled. Asha didn't want to think about President Amin today. Papa was still waiting to hear news about his Ugandan citizenship, and once he did, they'd be fine. Today was about Yesofu and the cricket match. Lost in her thoughts, Asha didn't hear the footsteps that crept up behind her.

"Move over!" Leela plopped down and handed Asha an Indian flag.

Asha waved a Ugandan flag. "I've already got one."

"You can't wave that," Neela said.

"Why?"

"Here we go again." Neela kicked off her sandals and stretched her legs out.

Asha opened her mouth to argue, but Neela cut her off.

"I know what you're going to say," Neela said smugly. "And you're wrong. Just because you were born here doesn't make you African."

"Come on," said Leela. "Can we not fight?"

Asha pushed down her anger. Neela always talked like she knew everything. Asha'd promised herself that she wasn't going to let anyone or anything ruin this day. She raised her arm and waved her Ugandan flag.

It was just the three of them today. Simon was with the

school cricket team, and some of their friends that usually sat with them at sport events had either left Entebbe or weren't coming.

"I've been looking for Yesofu. Have you seen him yet?" said Asha.

"I thought you were done with him," said Neela. "Or he was with you."

"No," Asha snapped, trying hard not to poke Neela with her flag. "We're still friends."

"Really, so you made up after that uniform mess?" Leela asked.

Asha looked away, her face growing hot. "Not exactly. Well, kind of."

"Which is it?" Neela looked at her.

"We're friends again. Okay."

"I've told you. You can't be friends with your servants." Neela sniffed.

Cheering swept across the park. A couple of players from the Ugandan team had come onto the field, and they huddled together in one corner. Yesofu was with them. He had on a new cricket uniform. Asha's cheeks grew hot, remembering his face when she gave him Rajeev's old uniform. She'd felt awful, especially when Fara told her that Yesofu'd saved up to buy a new one.

"Yesofu!" Asha stood, waving her arms. "Over here!"

He turned in her direction and waved back. He was still

waving when Akello walked up and clapped him on the back. A couple of weeks ago it would have been her down there on the field with him. Not Akello.

"Looks like Yesofu's with his new best friend," said Neela.

Asha sat down and let out a long breath.

"It was different when you guys were younger," said Leela. "But you're now . . ."

Asha crossed her arms. There was that word again. *Different*. She'd never given much thought to it before—opposites. Boy-girl. Black-brown. Rich-poor . . . she wasn't rich like those Indian families that lived on the hills in Kampala, but compared to Yesofu, yes. She'd never been to his place, but he talked about getting water from the well and having to share a room with Esi. Was she being foolish to think that those things didn't matter?

"Look!" Neela shouted.

Five soldiers stepped onto the field. Asha stood to get a better look. Dressed in their army fatigues, the soldiers marched together.

Arms straight.

Strides steady and even.

"Why would Idi Amin send his army here?" Asha asked.

Neela rolled onto her knees and stood. "Who knows why he does what he does."

"You sound just like Daddy," said Leela.

Across from Asha, another cluster of soldiers appeared.

They moved forward like a swarm of wasps, holding rifles tight against their chests. The crowd parted. Neela gasped next to her, and she felt Leela's fingers dig into her arm.

"Dada Amin," a woman cried out, and the crowd fell silent.

Stuck inside her TV at home, President Amin didn't seem so scary. But this man . . . this giant standing in front of Asha looked like he could crush her with a swipe of his hand.

17

YESOFU

THE PRESIDENT WAS here. Yesofu couldn't take his eyes off him. Idi Amin towered over everybody as he strutted onto the field. He wasn't right beside him, but Dada Amin was close enough for Yesofu to see all the medals that covered the front of his uniform. Not like one or two, but so many that the president almost glowed in the sunlight.

A crackling cut through the silence and then the Ugandan anthem boomed.

"*Ewe Uganda!*" Yesofu sang loudly. "*. . . Nchi ya uhuru.*" The land of freedom. "*Twaishi kwa amani na undugu.*" In peace and friendship we'll live. His voice choked and he stopped.

Freedom.

The people in his village were free. They worked as servants, drivers, cleaners because that's all there was for them. Was that really freedom? He looked at Baba and Mamma. President Amin was trying to change things for Africans. Yesofu wanted that for himself . . . for Mamma and Baba . . . for Esi and Akello. But also, Idi Amin was kicking out Indians. Kicking out Yesofu's friends. That didn't feel like living in peace and friendship. Everyone around him was singing, so he joined in.

As the final words of the national anthem were sung, cheers rose up. President Amin raised his hands to silence the crowd. He stepped up to the microphone at the edge of the field.

"Where's the Indian team?" His voice was loud and strong. "And they say Africans are always late." President Amin threw his head back, filling the air with laughter.

Yesofu looked around. He'd also been wondering what was keeping the other team. Did Dada Amin have something to do with them being late?

"You call me the hero of Africa." People started hushing one another as the president continued. "But it is you who are the real heroes of Uganda—our country. You who are born with the blood of Africa. With the heart of Africa."

Cheers rose up.

"These people, the shopkeepers, the landowners, the bankers, the government workers, they robbed us. They took our land and our jobs and have made us into servants. These

British and Indians. That is why they need to go."

The crowd cheered. Yesofu glanced toward the sidelines. Akello, Salim, and Yasid stood tall and straight, their eyes shining, like Dada Amin was the greatest in the whole wide world.

"I said a professional group could stay, but now I worry that those Indians remaining cannot serve the country in good spirit. So, this morning I made an announcement to my soldiers."

Yesofu gripped the ball tighter. There was silence throughout, as if the crowd took one giant breath together and then held it. Waiting.

"I revoked the exemption!" President Amin raised his fist into the air and shouted. "Sent the Indian team home." The cricket park exploded with cheers so thunderous that Yesofu could barely hear President Amin's voice over the crowd.

"Uganda belongs to us," President Amin continued. "I have taken back Ugandan citizenship from Indians. There is no room for Indians in Uganda! Let's play without them."

The noise of the crowd swelled. "Africa for Africans!" Yesofu turned to look out at the sea of hostile African faces staring at the area where most of the Indians were sitting.

Now everyone had to go. Asha. Coach. Simon. His whole cricket team. Yesofu wanted Dada Amin to help them get a better life. He wanted more for Baba and Mamma. But did Asha have to go for him to have a better future? He couldn't imagine her leaving and he couldn't imagine what it would be like if she stayed. How could he hang out with her? He'd look like a traitor to Dada Amin . . . to Akello and his friends.

President Amin walked closer to the crowd, smiling and waving.

"*Wahindi waende nyumbani!*" the crowds chanted.

In his head, Yesofu heard the words in English—*Indians go home.*

The crowd cried out. An Africa for Africans. One of the players from the Ugandan cricket team nudged Yesofu. He looked up. Sam Walusimbi. He was standing inches from his hero.

"An Africa for Africans!" Sam said to Yesofu.

The players' voices grew louder.

The crowd chanted and clapped. The sound was overpowering, like hundreds of beating *embuutu*—the big drums used for ceremonies or dances. Sam grinned at Yesofu and nudged him again. Yesofu smiled weakly. He opened his mouth and tried to join in the chanting. He tried, but the words stuck in his throat.

18

ASHA

"THERE IS NO room for Indians in Uganda!" President Amin raised his fist into the air.

Cheers and applause exploded. Asha repeated his words, feeling them ricochet back and forth inside her head.

Idi Amin couldn't just change his mind.

Not again.

Back and forth.

Go. Stay. Go. Stay.

She wished she could snap her fingers and make everything stop.

Had Papa been right all along? Was she foolish to think that President Amin would change his mind for good? She looked at the field, where Yesofu stood with the Ugandan team. If they left, she'd never see him again, and the thought scared her.

Leela clutched her stomach. "I feel sick."

Neela, her eyes full of panic, grabbed her sister's hand. "Let's find Mummy before you throw up." They took off, leaving Asha alone.

"*Wahindi waende nyumbani!*" the crowds chanted.

Those were the same words she'd heard that night in India Street. Today they chanted louder, in one unified voice. Like everyone . . . the Africans . . . had decided as a group that all Indians should go. She looked at Yesofu standing next to a Ugandan cricket player. Did he want her to leave too?

Mama rushed over and put her arm around Asha's shoulders. "Have you seen Papa?" Her eyes darted back and forth like a trapped animal. Her frown eased a little when she saw him hurrying toward them.

"Amin refused to allow the plane to land," Papa said. "He's sent the cricket team back to India." Papa started folding the chairs and stuffing mats into empty bags. "Pack up. Quickly."

"Why is President Amin doing this?" Asha asked.

"Not now!" Papa snapped.

Mama shook her head and pulled Asha close to her. "Help me put the food away."

Asha started closing the containers, but Papa snatched them from her hand and threw them into the basket. Samosas and vegetable pakoras spilled onto the picnic blanket. Asha leaned to pick up the fried pastries.

"Leave them," Papa barked. He gestured for Asha to start gathering the plates.

"*Wahindi waende nyumbani!*" the crowds continued chanting as the Ugandan team pounded their cricket bats into the ground, thumping an angry rhythm. The ground beneath Asha's feet seemed to tremble.

"Asha!" Mama waved her arms. "Hurry up."

All around, clusters of people scrambled to gather their belongings. Some children stood frozen, wide-eyed with fear. Others wailed as their parents grabbed their hands and tugged them out of the park. Panic. Fear. It was everywhere. Their neighbor Uma Auntie—Leela and Neela's aunt—struggled up the hill. Coach followed, lugging her basket. Asha started rolling up the woven mats.

"Leave it. Let's go!" Papa yanked Asha to her feet. Mama grabbed what she could hold and they ran toward the parking lot.

Asha struggled to keep up with Papa's long strides. She stumbled and Papa tightened his grip. Elbows and baskets jabbed at her as he dragged her into the jumble of cars, bicycles, and people rushing to get out. A car screeched to a halt as Papa ran in its path.

Horns blared.

Engines growled.

Asha felt like her heart was about to burst out of her body. Exhaust fumes burned her throat. She willed her legs to keep moving. To run faster. She wanted to get home, to her room. She'd be safe there. Away from the soldiers. Away from Idi Amin.

She scrambled into the back seat and barely shut the door before Papa pulled out of the parking lot. Asha spun around and looked back. The cheers continued . . . gradually getting quieter the farther they drove away.

"I knew he couldn't be trusted." Papa's voice sounded weary.

"This doesn't change anything," said Mama. "You have citizenship. We don't have to leave our home."

"This isn't just about a house . . . our things," said Papa. "It's about our children. Have you not seen the soldiers? Seen the guns they point at our children like it's—it's some kind of joke?"

"Enough, Ashok! Nothing has happened to anyone's child. Nothing. All this rubbish with Amin will pass."

"Thousands of applications for citizenship have been canceled. Nine years some of them have been waiting for their citizenship to go through. Since independence."

"What are you saying?" Mama asked.

"I've been waiting to get final word on my citizenship

papers. Now we know it's been revoked. We are running out of time. And the British . . . you think they will allow all of us in? No, Mira, we need to leave. Now."

Asha stared out the window at the green hills. Papa may be ready to go, but she wasn't.

≈ 19 ≈

YESOFU

THE VILLAGE BUZZED with excitement, gathering to sing and dance the traditional *nankasa* and *bakisimba*. It didn't matter that not everyone in the village was part of the Ganda tribe. Today they joined together as a group to celebrate. An Africa for Africans. Yesofu picked up two empty pails and headed to the well, his feet moving to the beat of the *embuutu* and *engalabi* drums. He wanted to feel the same thrill that Akello, Salim, and Yasid felt over the president's news, but he couldn't get Asha out of his head. He'd even tried to join in their celebrations, worried how it would look to his friends if he didn't. They were his brothers, his family. It felt like he was betraying them by not joining in, but wrong if he did.

Akello's feet came scuffing through the grass toward him.

"Why do you look like you've been sucking on raw mangos?" Akello made a sour face.

"I was thinking about what President Amin said today."

Akello was looking at him funny. "You're thinking about Asha."

Of course he was. She didn't deserve to be kicked out. Overhead clouds were building. A flock of tiny birds swooped and dove into the bushes, disappearing into the darkness. Yesofu glanced at Akello as they zigzagged past the old ground well up to the central well with the hand pump. The tall elephant grass surrounding the village crackled like the thoughts in his head. If he couldn't be real with Akello, then who? Yesofu took a deep breath. "You know what I think?"

"What?" Akello set his pail under the spout, placed both hands on the long handle, and pulled down hard.

Yesofu hesitated, and then plunged on before he lost his courage. "I think that . . . things could change . . . I mean, they can change without getting rid of all the Indians."

From deep inside the well, a gurgling rumbled beneath Yesofu's feet.

"You don't get it . . . do you?" Akello's arm pumped up and down. "This is our land. They don't belong here." Water gushed out of the spout. "Asha lives in her big house. She goes to fancy dances at her club. She doesn't have to worry about money. She doesn't have to quit school." Akello stopped suddenly.

96

"Neither do you," said Yesofu. "I can ask Baba to talk to your dad."

"It won't matter. It's the only way we'll be ready."

"For what?" Yesofu pulled down on the pump and water spilled into the pail.

"Once the Indians go, there'll be land to buy . . . shops for sale." Akello picked up the second pail of water and handed it to Yesofu. Thunder rumbled overhead and they quickly started down the hill.

"So you're okay taking from the Indians?" he challenged Akello.

"Why not?"

"I don't know. It just doesn't feel right." Yesofu imagined Kintu at Café Nile. He'd worked for Mr. Bhatt for years. Bet he wished he could own his own café. But was it right to kick out Mr. Bhatt and give Café Nile to Kintu?

"It's not like I'd be stealing," said Akello.

"In a way . . ." Their eyes met, each daring the other to back down.

"You want Asha to stay. But did you ever think that it may not be good for her?"

"What do you mean?"

"She's your friend. I get that." Akello stopped in front of his place. "But she needs to go. Her Uganda is changing. It's going to be an Africa for Africans. Not an Africa for Indians and Africans."

Rain tapped on the iron-sheeted roofs, making a racket as loud as all the noise in Yesofu's head. He tried to make sense of everything as he walked back to his hut. *Staying may not be good for Asha.* But he couldn't imagine his life without her. Who would help him make sense of those long, boring stories in English class? Who would help him find the best banana leaves that always won the downhill races? Who would save extra samosas for him when the Entebbe Institute had big parties? Who'd laugh at his jokes? The rain was coming down harder now. Yesofu hurried. Uganda may be changing, but that didn't mean all Indians had to leave. Staying would be good for Asha.

He was right. He was sure of it.

≋20≋
ASHA

"WHAT AM I going to do?" Asha asked Teelu. She'd snuck into Papa's office to make the long-distance call to her sister in London. "Everyone is starting to leave. Our neighbors. Kids at school and at the club. And now Papa wants us to go too."

Two weeks had passed since the cricket match. Thirty-six days remaining, the radio announcer had shouted from Fara's static-filled radio at breakfast this morning. The newspaper on Papa's desk confirmed the countdown. Asha had to figure out how to stop Papa before he made them leave.

"You have to help, Teelu. Papa went to the bank yesterday to apply for travel vouchers. He almost got them too, but couldn't because he needed different paperwork."

"Where are Papa and Mama?"

"In the sitting room with Mr. Gupta and Coach and his parents." Asha had woken this morning to everyone arriving at the house. "Teelu, you have to help me figure out a way to convince Papa to stay."

"Listen, Asha . . ."

"Wait." Asha cut her off. Whenever Teelu started a sentence with *listen, Asha*, it usually meant she was about to say something Asha wouldn't like. "If you're going to say I should listen to Papa, then I am hanging up."

Teelu sighed. "Do you remember when you had nightmares and would run to my room in the middle of the night?"

"Yes. You'd tell me stories of Ganesh so I'd go back to sleep." Ganesh was the chubby, gentle, wise elephant-headed Hindu god known to remove obstacles. Leela and Neela had given Asha a small statue of him as a gift. President Amin was the biggest obstacle in her life right now. His big, round face stared at Asha from the front page of the *Uganda Argus* as her sister blabbed in her ear. Mr. Gupta had written an article about President Amin hurting Uganda by making Indians leave. Asha picked up a blue pen and scribbled on the president's face. "I'm not a little kid anymore, Teelu," Asha interrupted.

"I know," Teelu continued. "I learned something new about Ganesh from my Hindu friend."

100

Asha scrunched up the newspaper and threw it across the room. "What?"

"She told me that Ganesh also places obstacles in the path of those who need to be checked, to stop us from doing things without thinking it through . . ."

Asha stopped listening. Sitting under the newspaper were two passports belonging to Papa and Mama. At sixteen, Asha would get her own passport, but for now, she could travel under Mama's—not that she'd ever thought she would need to. Papa had probably taken the passports out when he went to apply for their travel vouchers and forgot to put them away. Ganesh had given her what she needed to remove the obstacle in her way. Without the passports they couldn't leave, and even though Papa worked for the ministry of tourism, it would still take time to get new ones. Time for someone to stop President Amin.

"Asha. Are you there? Hello?" Teelu's voice pulled Asha back to the phone.

"Yes. I'm listening and you're right." She picked up the passports and shoved them inside the pocket of her school skirt.

"London isn't so bad once you get used to it."

"Yeah. Okay. Look, I have to go. I'll see you when you come home."

"No, Asha, wait."

101

Asha hung up. She heard voices. It sounded like people were leaving. She couldn't let Papa find her inside his office. She quickly slipped out and darted upstairs to her bedroom. She needed a good hiding place for the passports. Somewhere nobody would find them, especially Fara. She was up here cleaning every day and would find them under the mattress or tucked in her clothes. She needed to put them inside something . . . like a case. She saw her carrom bag sitting on her desk. It was perfect. Asha opened up the leather ten-inch square bag and slipped the passports inside among the black-and-tan round discs, pulling the drawstring tightly. She looked at the tall wardrobe with all her clothes. On the bottom shelf, her sandals and shoes lay in a tumbled mess, but the next shelf up was a stack of sweaters. She tucked the carrom bag behind them. She smiled at herself in the mirror. Already relieved.

"Asha!" Fara called out from downstairs. "Hurry up. You'll be late for school."

Asha slipped on her shoes and ran downstairs. As she passed the sitting room, she heard Mama.

"I wish you wouldn't get involved."

Her voice sounded tense, and Asha pictured Mama wringing the edge of her *dupatta* in her hands, tighter and tighter.

"I have to," said Papa. "People we know are trying to get out. Their passports are being confiscated. They can only buy tickets using Uganda shillings—no other currency—and they need written approval from the Bank of Uganda. . . . Applications are stacked . . . the deadline is approaching. Amin is getting more and more dangerous."

"Exactly," said Mama. "Anyone suspected of disloyalty to President Amin is being . . ."

Mama's voice cracked and quieted, and Asha heard two words. ". . . too risky."

Risky? What was Papa doing? Asha stepped closer and the floor creaked beneath her feet. The voices stopped. Every muscle in her body froze. Mama's *sari* rustled and footsteps shuffled closer. If Asha ran, they'd hear her and know she'd been eavesdropping. She held herself still. After a minute, the conversation continued and she relaxed.

"What if something goes wrong?" Mama asked.

"It won't."

"You don't know that for sure."

"You're right," said Papa. "I don't."

A pang of fear shot through Asha. Papa worked at the tourism office. Was he helping people get out of Uganda? The president wanted Indians gone. He should be happy Papa was helping them leave. It had to be something else— but what? Footsteps clomped up the verandah steps. She looked up, surprised to see Esi.

"Open up," he called through the screen door.

Asha hurried over and pushed open the door. Esi held a sack of rice in his arms and stumbled inside, pretending to collapse from the weight.

"*Asante*," Esi thanked her. He paused and looked at Asha. "What are you up to?"

Asha felt her face get hot. "What? I'm not doing anything."

BANG! Mama or Papa had shut the door to the sitting room.

Esi's eyebrow shot up. "Not listening in on your parents?"

"What? No." Asha hurried toward the kitchen, Esi following.

"Here's the rice, Mamma," he said as he stepped into the kitchen.

"*Asante sana*," Fara thanked him. She shook her wet hands over the sink and gestured with her chin toward the cupboard. "Put it there."

Fara wiped her wet hands on her apron and smiled at Asha. "There's my *malaika*," she said, greeting Asha with her special nickname.

"I thought I was your angel," Esi said, and stuck out his bottom lip, pretending to pout. Esi was joking, but Asha wondered if he and Yesofu ever got jealous about having to share Fara. She was like a second mother to Teelu and Asha. Did that bother them?

Fara gave Esi a playful pinch on his ear. "You're my *shetani*."

Devil. Asha laughed. Esi hooked his two fingers on his head like horns and rushed at Fara. She swatted him with the wet dish towel, but he snatched it away and wrapped his arms around her shoulders.

Asha picked up her lunch tiffin that Fara had prepared and said goodbye to Fara and Esi. On her way out the door, she glanced upstairs, feeling a tiny twinge of something—guilt. Doubt. Worry. She thought of having to leave her home and pushed aside her uncertainty. She'd done the right thing taking the passports. And with that thought, Asha stepped out onto the verandah, breathing in the sweet-smelling bougainvillea and hibiscus bushes.

≋21≋
YESOFU

IN THE DISTANCE, Yesofu heard a loud clanging—the warning bell—and broke into a sprint. He pulled open the door and stepped inside just as the final bell rang, almost running into Cecil, a younger primary class five student. Extra desks and kids crammed inside, filling every space, so that he couldn't even walk through without bumping into someone. Coach stood in his usual spot with his back to the class, writing on the board. From the opposite side of the room, Asha waved. She'd saved him his usual seat behind her, which was a good thing because every other seat was taken.

Who was Akello to tell him he had to pick between his Indian and African friends? He just wanted Yesofu to dump

Asha and Simon. It wasn't happening.

"So, what's going on?" He pointed around. "Why are there are so many kids?"

Leela leaned over. "They combined the different classes."

"Not enough teachers," Asha added.

Neela looked at Yesofu. "President Amin made them leave." She pulled her book out of her bag and dropped it onto her desk.

Yesofu locked his jaw, determined not to let Neela get to him. He hated how she made him feel like he was somehow responsible for what was happening at their school. Neela looked like a rose, but she was all pokey and prickly. Yesofu didn't understand how she and Leela were twins.

A wadded piece of paper hit Yesofu in the back of the head and he turned. Oh man. How was this possible? The class was divided. And he was the only African on this side of the room. In the far-left corner by the bookcase, he saw Akello, glaring. Yesofu lifted his hand to wave, until he saw the empty desk behind Akello. He turned around, wishing that he'd looked around before sitting by Asha. Behind him, Salim and Yasid chuckled. Yesofu felt his face get hot. He gripped the edge of his seat. He didn't think sitting with Asha and Simon was wrong, but still he felt like a traitor.

"Quiet down," said Coach Edwin, flipping through the pages in his text. "I want students in primary classes four and five to get started on their math. Students in primary classes six and seven, take out your maps. We're going to review geography."

Neela cleared her throat. She raised her hand and blurted out, "Is it true the president can make all Indians leave?"

All eyes turned toward Neela. Yesofu sank lower in his chair, wondering if he could make it to the empty desk behind Akello without the whole class noticing. Coach ignored Neela and called on Simon to read. Simon stared at his book, saying nothing. Yesofu kicked the leg of Simon's desk.

"Is there a problem?" Coach looked around the class.

"Um," stammered Simon. "Is it true . . . what Neela said about the president?"

Not Simon too. Why did all this have to get in the way of school? He'd never be ready for the end of primary exams. Or secondary school.

"It's true," said Salim.

"He already is making you leave," added Yasid. "You don't belong here."

"That's crazy," said Leela. "We've lived here just as long as you."

Coach tugged at his tie. "Let's move on."

"It doesn't matter if we were born here," said Simon. "He wants us out and we have to go." He stopped like the words were stuck in his throat. "My family's leaving once our travel vouchers for the United States come in."

What? The United States was thousands and thousands of miles away. When had this happened? Simon hadn't said anything when they were at practice yesterday.

From the back, Akello called out, "He's not the only one."

Yesofu squashed even lower, wishing his desk could swallow him.

Asha twisted around. "We're Ugandans. Just like you." She clutched the edge of her desk, her hands trembling. "And we're not going anywhere."

"You are, Asha," Akello shot back. "Amin is getting rid of *all* of you."

Yesofu looked back and forth between his two friends—Asha and Akello—wondering how he could stop this battle without looking like he was taking sides.

"That's enough!" Coach shouted.

"I don't have to listen to you." Akello jumped up. His chair fell and clattered on the floor.

Everyone stared at Akello. Coach's jaw tightened. He pushed his way to the back of the class and grabbed Akello's arm. "I said that's enough." His words were thick with anger. "This is a classroom. Not some cricket field."

"*Usiniguse!*" Akello wrenched his arm free. "Don't touch me!" He reached the door in two strides and paused. He locked eyes on Yesofu before walking out. "Goodbye, Indians."

It was like Akello had sucked all the air out of the room.

Wham! Salim knocked over his chair and walked out.

Wham! Yasid did the same.

Wham! Wham! Wham! Other Africans left. Yesofu sat up straighter. He wanted to join Akello and the others, but he also couldn't disrespect Coach—or leave Asha and Simon. Yesofu looked at the empty seats on the opposite side of the class. *Should he go?* Coach moved quickly and shut the door. It was too late. Only Yesofu and one other African remained. He shrank down in his seat.

Coach didn't say anything more about President Amin or Indians having to leave.

"Open your books and get back to your math and geography."

Yesofu nudged Asha's chair with his foot, but she refused to look at him. He stared at his book, the words blurring into thin, black lines. He was wrong thinking he could juggle his two groups of friends.

Indian or African. Friends or family.

It didn't matter which one he picked. He lost either way.

22

ASHA

SCHOOL FINALLY ENDED, and Asha darted outside, desperate to escape the suffocating classroom. After Akello left, she'd tried to concentrate, but couldn't. Akello had gone, but his words had stayed, hidden in the corners of the classroom like black mold—*Amin is getting rid of all of you.*

Asha glanced at the banyan tree where she and Yesofu usually met after school. She couldn't remember the last time they'd walked home together. It had to be right before President Amin announced he wanted Indians to leave Uganda. She missed racing to see who could beat the other home to get first dibs on what Fara had waiting for tea. A group of kids walked by, laughing and talking. She hoisted her backpack onto her shoulder and started home.

Asha slowed as she rounded the corner onto Lugado Street and started counting the growing number of empty homes of Indians who had left. "Five, six, seven . . ." When she got to a dozen, she stopped, worried that the next house would be theirs. Was Akello right . . . was she next?

She thought about the two passports she had hidden inside the leather bag with her carrom game pieces, wondering if Papa'd looked for them after she'd left. Even if he hadn't today, it was only a matter of time. Asha continued, and stopped when she reached Uma Auntie's house. Leela and Neela's aunt, Mr. Gupta's sister, had lived next door to Asha's family since Mama and Papa were first married. She'd left last week and gone back to Bombay. It was strange seeing her chair sitting empty on the front porch. Asha heard a rustling from the oleander bushes along the fence. Suddenly Yesofu jumped out and ran at her.

"Aghhhhhhhh!"

Asha yelped and nearly jumped out of her skin. She flung her backpack at him. "What are you doing here?"

Yesofu shrugged. "It's been a while."

Asha narrowed her eyes. "And whose fault is that?"

"I get it. You're mad about Akello, but what did you want me to do?"

"Say something. Make him stop." Asha paused and looked down. "Stand up for me."

"How? What'd you want me to say?"

112

"Tell Akello he's wrong."

"It's not that easy."

Silence settled between them. Asha bent down to get her backpack, but Yesofu picked it up and swung it over his shoulder. She looked at him and took a deep breath. "I'm just scared that I'm going to have to leave Entebbe. This is my home."

Yesofu didn't say a word, but his eyes never left her face as he dropped both backpacks and wrapped his arms around her. It was better than anything he could have said. After a few seconds, he let go.

"What do you think Mamma's cooked for tea?"

"Vegetable pakoras." Asha smiled and then took off running. "Race you home," she shouted over her shoulder.

It didn't take long for Yesofu to catch up, and they ran into the garden at the same time. A loud bang caught Asha's attention. "Did you hear that?" she asked.

Yesofu pointed to the servants' house. "It came from over there."

"But that door's always locked." Asha cautiously approached the shack. A few feet away, she stopped in her tracks. The door was open—just a crack.

Yesofu stumbled into her. "What's wrong?"

"Look." Asha pointed. "It's open. No padlock." She put her finger to her lips and continued through the dried twigs and leaves, treading carefully to avoid making any noise.

Yesofu put his hand on her arm and she stopped.

"Let me go first." He stepped around her and slowly crept up to the door. She followed closely behind, careful not to step on the backs of his sandals. They crouched outside and listened.

"I don't hear anything." Yesofu nudged the wooden door and it creaked open.

Asha peered over his shoulder. The front room was empty, but suddenly a noise—like someone moving around—came from the back room.

"Who's there?" Yesofu called out.

Silence.

"Now what?" said Asha.

Yesofu gestured with his chin and stepped inside. Asha followed right behind. Light from outside poured through the open door into the empty room. She walked toward the back room.

"We know you're in there," said Yesofu. "Come out."

Asha clasped the doorknob firmly and turned. The door was locked. She twisted again. The knob rattled. A loud crash came from the other side of the door. Asha leapt back. Yesofu reached out and grabbed her hand. They darted out of the shack, running back along the path. Asha struggled to keep up as they scrambled around the side of the house and onto the verandah. They sat on the steps, catching their breath, when a sudden rumble filled the air. The clank and grind of something big and mechanical, unlike any sound Asha'd heard before. She looked up as a military tank ground to a halt right in front of her house.

23

YESOFU

THE TANK RUMBLED and shook, rattling the windows. It was huge, with a long, narrow gun on top, three times the size of a cricket bat. Yesofu had seen tanks driving on the hills surrounding Kampala toward Makindye Prison. But never one in town. Definitely not this close.

Screeching tires swallowed his words. An open pickup truck swerved into the neighbor's driveway where Leela and Neela's aunt used to live. Before the truck came to a complete stop, soldiers, with rifles bouncing against their chests, jumped out and rushed up to the house. Yesofu's heart pounded. Another soldier stepped into Asha's yard. He wore a fierce expression and clutched the rifle strapped to his chest.

"You there!" He pointed at Asha. "Get your parents."

Asha stood next to Yesofu staring at the soldier, barely breathing. He nudged her.

"Th-th-they're not home." Her voice squeaked like it was about to break.

The soldier took a step forward and pointed at her. "Come here."

Yesofu went to put his arm around Asha, but in that second, the soldier grabbed Asha, dragging her away. "Hey! What are you doing?"

"*Nyamaza!*" Yesofu obeyed and shut up. The soldier pulled Asha onto her tiptoes until his nose was inches from hers. "Where are they?"

"I—I—I don't know."

Asha's voice shook so badly Yesofu could hardly understand her. He stared at the soldier, feeling a mix of hate and fear. He wanted to rush inside and get Mamma, but he was too afraid of what might happen if he looked away. "Mamma!" he shouted. There was no response from inside the house.

Yesofu could see Asha's lower lip starting to tremble. He had to do something. The soldier had a tight grip on her arm and didn't look like he was about to release her. Yesofu took a step closer. "Let her go!" He clenched his hands to stop his fingers from trembling. "She hasn't done anything. You can't come here and—"

The soldier shoved Asha to the ground. Yesofu rushed

toward her. At that same moment, the screen door burst open and Mamma ran out, her springy collection of braids shaking from her haste. As Yesofu looked over at Asha, he felt a hand grab the back of his shirt. He was yanked so hard that his feet lifted right off the ground.

"Why are you helping these Indians?" the soldier demanded, his voice thick with disgust. He spat into the dirt.

"She's my friend." Yesofu took a breath and felt his confidence building.

The soldier leaned in, his face so close, Yesofu could smell his breath. It reeked of cigarettes and he almost gagged.

"You need to learn what it means to be African," snarled the soldier.

Yesofu didn't need a lesson in patriotism. Not from this guy. Yesofu felt himself being dragged out of the garden. He kicked his legs, digging his heels into the dirt. Twisting. Wriggling. Anything to escape. The soldier squeezed his arm hard. "Do you want me to break it off?"

"Let him go."

It was Asha, her voice barely more than a whisper. Yesofu thought the soldier hadn't heard. But then his head snapped in Asha's direction.

"Shut up!" His eyes narrowed and the vein in his neck pulsed. "You're a filthy Indian. The sooner you're gone the better."

Asha was standing now. Mamma walked over and pulled

her closer like she was one of her own children. "You heard the girl. Let my son go."

Yesofu knew that tone. Mamma meant business, but going up against this soldier was dangerous. Yesofu wriggled to get free, but the hold on him tightened. Out of the corner of his eye, he saw a flash. The soldier had pulled out his gun.

24

ASHA

ASHA GULPED AT the air as if each breath would fill her with the strength to rush forward and save Yesofu. Before she could move, the beeping of a horn punctured the tension. A wave of relief washed over her as Esi motored down the road. He'd make the soldiers leave. Esi screeched to a halt, inches from Mama's roses, and jumped off his motorbike. He looked back and forth between Fara and the soldier holding Yesofu.

"Let him go," Esi demanded.

"Stay out of this." The soldier glared at Esi and twisted Yesofu's arm.

Fara pulled Asha closer. "Go inside and get my bag."

"I don't want to leave."

"Just do it!"

Fara's face hardened, and Asha knew better than to argue. She ran to the kitchen. She snatched Fara's woven bag off the nail where it always hung and darted back outside. The soldier still held Yesofu against him and was waving his gun around as he fired words at Esi.

"He's my brother." Esi pulled Yesofu out of the soldier's grip. "Not a traitor."

Esi and the soldier stood facing one another, their angry words blasting like bullets. Another soldier appeared. In one big stride, he stepped up to Esi and jabbed him in the shoulder.

Asha ran over and gave Fara her bag. She took it and walked straight up to the two soldiers. She said something Asha couldn't hear and began rummaging in her bag. Fara held out her hand. The yelling stopped. The sun glittered off the shiny coins and bills in her palm. The soldier snatched the money from Fara's hand and marched away.

"Let's go!" The soldiers climbed onto the back of the pickup truck. The vehicles growled to life, and they drove off.

Asha hurried over to where Yesofu stood with Fara and Esi.

Before she could say anything, Esi grabbed Yesofu by the shirt collar and shook him. "Are you mad?"

Yesofu looked completely bewildered. "W-w-what do you mean?"

"Putting yourself in danger like that." Esi glared at Yesofu. "What's wrong with you?"

Asha stared at Esi. Her temper stirred and she had to bite down on her lips to stop her words from flying out of her mouth. Yesofu was only trying to help. That's how he was. And Esi was the same way. If anyone should understand why Yesofu had stepped in to help her, she thought it would have been him. He'd done the same thing that day he pulled her out of the crowd in India Street when she got separated from Leela and Neela.

Esi shook Yesofu. "Do you know what could have happened?"

"I had to—" Yesofu swallowed. "He had Asha."

"Leave him alone," said Fara.

"No, Mamma!" Esi spoke fiercely. "This isn't a game. These soldiers won't think twice about who they kill."

Fara came over and put her hand on Esi's arm. "Enough. Let him go," she said softly. She stood between all of them—Asha, Yesofu, and Esi. Then she sank to the ground, her dark eyes spilling with tears. Asha wanted to wrap her arms around her *ayah*.

"*Usijali*," said Yesofu.

Fara wiped her eyes with the edge of her apron.

"Yesofu's right. It's okay." Asha tried to keep the quiver of uncertainty out of her voice.

"No, we need to listen to Esi."

"*Nasikitika*," Yesofu said softly.

Asha wanted to tell him that he didn't need to be sorry, but she had no words in her.

Fara pulled Asha and Yesofu to her, hugging them together in her usual way. But today it felt different, as if she might never let go.

30 DAYS

25

ASHA

ASHA RAISED HER face to catch the slight breeze rustling through the branches of the jacaranda tree. It was lunch, and she sat with Simon, Leela, and Neela under the shade of the purple tree out on the school playground. So far Simon's family hadn't got their travel papers, but Asha knew it was only a matter of time. Not asking, or not knowing when, meant she could almost pretend he wasn't leaving.

"Have you seen Yesofu?" Asha asked. She took a bite of her sweet mango slice.

"Yesofu," sniffed Neela. "He's just like the rest of them."

Asha remembered how Yesofu had stood up to the soldier. "You're wrong," she snapped. "He's different."

"I wouldn't be so sure," said Leela. "Yesofu has been hanging out more with Yasid and Salim."

Asha swallowed wrong and coughed—not Leela too.

"He can't help it," said Simon. "He has to stick with his own kind." He popped his last bite in his mouth and licked his fingers. "Especially now."

It didn't matter what Simon said. She knew how Yesofu really felt. He wouldn't have stepped in to help if he wasn't really her friend. She drifted back into the conversation.

"President Amin isn't just crazy." Simon's voice dropped to a whisper. "He's a monster."

"That's rubbish," said Neela, and kicked off her sandals, wriggling her pink polished toes.

Simon shook his head. "He makes people disappear."

"What do you mean?" Asha leaned in closer.

"Amin arrests anyone he thinks is against him and then . . ." Simon swiped his finger across his neck and let his head fall to the side. "Their bodies are chopped up and fed to the crocodiles."

"You're making that up," said Neela.

"It's true," said Simon.

Asha shivered. It was well known that farther down the river, crocodiles lurked on the edges. Was Amin making people disappear? Was he throwing dead bodies into the lake? The thought made her sick to her stomach.

"But we don't have to worry. Papa and his friends are

sorting things out." He nudged Asha with his elbow. "Right, Asha?"

"What?"

"You know . . ." Simon leaned closer. "Our dads are working with their friends against Amin, for good."

"You don't know what you're talking about," Neela said to Simon. "Daddy writes for the *Uganda Argus*. He's not working against the president or anyone."

"But he tells it like it is," said Simon. "That makes the president mad."

As Neela and Simon argued back and forth, Asha thought more about what Simon said. Papa disagreed with President Amin, but he wouldn't put himself in danger. Or would he? It was odd he hadn't said anything about the missing passports, but if he wasn't thinking about leaving, then he wouldn't need them. Was Simon right? *Too dangerous.* The words slammed into her head like a charging rhino.

The warning bell rang and kids started moving toward the school doors. As the crowds cleared, Asha spotted Yesofu walking toward the school with Akello. She hadn't seen Akello since that day he stormed out. Things had been better between her and Yesofu with Akello not around. Hopefully he hadn't changed his mind and decided to come back.

"Yesofu!" she called out.

He looked up and she waved. He tossed something in the bin and jogged over. Akello lingered a few feet behind him.

"*Habari*," said Simon.

"What's up?" said Yesofu.

"We're talking about your president." Neela tossed back her hair. "And how he's killing people and chopping them up."

"Where'd you hear that?" Yesofu glared at her.

"Simon," said Neela.

"It's a lie," said Yesofu. "You make Dada Amin sound like a monster. He's helping us."

"You mean you." Neela shook her head. "He's not helping Indians. He's ruining our lives."

"How come you're so quiet?" Akello looked right at Asha.

She held her hand over her eyes, blocking the glare of the sun. "Well, I don't like that he wants all Indians to leave, but . . ."

"I told you." Akello's voice swelled. "She's like all the other Indians. They only care about themselves." He stepped closer to Yesofu. "Not like you and me."

Asha jumped up, her words impossible to hold inside. "I don't want to be like you, Akello. Nobody does! You're a *shamba* boy . . . working in the fields. You're nothing!"

The anger in Akello's eyes disappeared as a smug grin spread across his face.

Oh, no. No. Asha's words burned her mouth. Yesofu's father worked in the fields. So did Yesofu. She placed her hand on Yesofu's arm. "I d-d-didn't mean it like that," she stammered.

Yesofu shook off her hand. "How did you mean it? *Baba* isn't nothing."

"I wasn't talking about him." Asha's mind scrambled, trying to think of what she could say to fix this.

"What about me?" Yesofu asked. He looked at Asha with the same hurt in his eyes as the night of her birthday party.

"Forget her," Akello scoffed. "Let's go."

Asha watched Yesofu walk away with Akello, fighting the urge to run after him. It wouldn't make a difference anyway. There was nothing she could say to make it better.

≈26≈
YESOFU

AFTER SCHOOL, YESOFU took off. This morning Mamma had given him a list and asked him to stop at Evergreen Grocers and Provisions Mart. On the long hot miles to India Street, Yesofu tossed his cricket ball up and down. *Shamba boy. Nothing.* He clutched his ball tightly. She'd sounded like the other Indians, looking down their noses at Africans. And she called herself his best friend.

Yesofu turned onto India Street and stopped. It was like he'd walked into another universe. Half the shops were shut. Rolling gates covered the front windows and rusted padlocks chained the doors. Yesofu peered through the window of Eagle Shoe Center. Boots, sandals, slippers, and heels lined the shelves, but there was no sign of the Indian shopkeeper.

He counted how many shops had closed. Four. Five. Six. He stopped at the shop where he'd bought his cricket uniform. Its windows were smashed and inside the shelves were empty. This didn't feel like opportunity waiting.

Across the street, a woman stood holding a small girl. Two soldiers stepped out of a shop, dragging an Indian man by the arms. A soldier motioned for the woman to put down the girl. As soon as she set the child down, the soldier grabbed her and pulled her against him. The man, his face red as his turban, fired a rapid slew of words. The soldier spun around and hit him with the butt of his rifle. The man staggered backward and fell.

Yesofu's heart thumped, making it hard to breathe. He clutched his cricket ball to his chest. These soldiers seemed even more vicious than the ones at Asha's. He stared at the bleeding man lying in the street and wondered if President Amin knew what his soldiers were doing. The woman who had been holding the girl rushed toward the man. The little girl screamed, pulling at her mother's *sari*. A soldier shouted, his rifle inches from the man's forehead.

Yesofu couldn't stand here doing nothing. He went to take a step forward, but then he remembered Esi's warning and stopped. Mamma wasn't here to save him this time, and there was no telling what these soldiers would do. Yesofu looked up and down India Street. The cries of the man and woman were piercing. He had to get out of here. Mr. Kapoor's shop

133

was nearby. He started running. Eyes down. Legs pumping. *Be open. Be open.* Sale signs covered the front window of Evergreen Grocers and Provisions Mart. Yesofu pushed the door and fell inside. His cricket ball dropped, rolling across the floor.

"Yesofu?"

It was Mr. Gomez. Asha's dad stood with Mr. Kapoor at the counter. Yesofu tried to speak, but his words caught in his throat.

"What's wrong?" Mr. Gomez rushed over. "Are you hurt?"

Yesofu's breath came in short gasps.

"*Pole pole.*" Mr. Gomez put his hands on Yesofu's shoulders. "Slowly. Take a breath."

The warmth of Mr. Gomez's hands eased Yesofu's panic. He pointed outside. "Soldiers everywhere. They're beating him. It's awful. I didn't know what to do—"

"It's not your fault," said Mr. Gomez.

"Come, sit down." Mr. Kapoor pointed to a wooden stool.

Mr. Gomez led Yesofu over. "You shouldn't be in town. The commissioner and soldiers are checking all the shops to make sure owners have immigration papers or identity cards. If they don't, well . . ." He glanced at Mr. Kapoor and stopped.

Yesofu caught the look between them. Did Mr. Kapoor have his papers? He dug out the crumpled shopping list from his pocket.

Mr. Kapoor shook his head. "I've stopped filling the shelves. My family already left back to India. I should be leaving soon."

"I'll take what you have," said Yesofu.

"Give me a minute." Mr. Kapoor disappeared into the storage room.

"How come you're here?" Yesofu asked Asha's dad. "Usually Mamma does the shopping."

Mr. Gomez got up and peered out the window. His forehead wrinkled in the same way that Baba's did whenever he was worried. "Um, yes."

Mr. Kapoor came out with a bag. "I found some sugar, but no flour, salt, or spices. With all the Indians closing up shop, supplies are running low everywhere."

"You better lock up and go." Asha's dad cut off Mr. Kapoor. "I'll be in touch."

Mr. Kapoor thrust the bag at Yesofu. "Don't worry about paying."

"Come on." Mr. Gomez led Yesofu outside. "Don't hang around. Here's money for the bus. Go straight home." With those final words, he turned and hurried off.

On the bus ride home, Yesofu wondered at the real reason why Mr. Gomez was in the shop. He wasn't buying supplies. That was for sure. The bus pulled into its last stop and Yesofu walked the short distance home. The steady thumping, *thad-da, thad-da,* of heavy, wooden pestles quieted

Asha's words—*shamba boy*—and his questions about Mr. Gomez and Mr. Kapoor. Everything in his village looked normal. Firewood smoked and crackled beneath pots of bubbling stews. Salim's twin brothers, Wemusa and Wasswa ran around barefoot, chasing one another. Akello's sisters were heading to the well, swinging empty pails in their hands. It was exactly like it should be.

Unchanged.

Safe from soldiers.

Later that night, Yesofu practiced cricket with Akello and Yasid. The ugliness of the day slid off him and into the red dirt as they tossed the ball back and forth. Here, on this makeshift field, he belonged. Here, he mattered. Here, he didn't have to hide in the kitchen or come through back doors.

"Heard you saw some soldiers taking care of an Indian man," said Akello.

Yesofu shivered. "Beating him." He reached his arm back and threw the ball.

"He got what's coming," said Akello.

Yesofu looked at Yasid. He looked as shocked as Yesofu. Neither of them said a word. A couple of weeks ago Akello had been bugging Yesofu for ignoring Asha because she'd broken her birthday bracelet. Now he was all for soldiers beating Indians.

"You don't mean that," said Yesofu.

"Don't tell me what I mean and what I don't," Akello shot back. "That Indian probably deserved it."

"Not all of them."

"Really?" Akello asked. "What about Asha calling you a filthy *shamba* boy?"

"I'm mad at her, but I'm not going to beat her up." Yesofu didn't want to think about Asha or any other Indians. He just wanted to play cricket and forget about it all. He tossed the ball to Yasid.

"I've got you covered." Akello winked at Yesofu. "We're real friends. And real friends take care of each other."

An uneasy feeling crept up the back of Yesofu's neck. Yasid sent the ball spinning. Yesofu missed and it flew into the shrubs.

"I'll get it," said Akello, and took off.

Yasid hurried over. "Listen." He glanced in Akello's direction.

"What?"

"Akello's mad . . . like really angry at Asha for making fun of you guys."

"He has every right to be."

"He's gonna get her back for what she said."

Yesofu rubbed the back of his neck. Lately, Akello strutted around like he was one of Dada Amin's soldiers, blaming everything wrong in his life on Indians. He hated them. But this was Asha. Sure, he had every right to be mad at her for calling them *shamba boys.* Yesofu was mad too, but not enough to do something stupid.

He's gonna get her back for what she said. Akello sauntered out of the bushes. He smiled and tossed the ball to Yesofu.

Akello knew what Asha was like.

He knew she had a temper.

He wouldn't hurt her—would he?

27

ASHA

A WHOLE WEEK. And Yesofu still refused to have anything to do with her. Asha wanted so much to talk to him and apologize for what she'd said, but at lunch and breaks, he hung out with Yasid and Salim. He'd even switched seats, moving to the opposite side of the classroom into Akello's empty desk.

Today Asha was one of the first to get to school, and she snagged the only seat by the window. Even after combining classes four, five, six, and seven, the room felt empty. The principal appeared at the door at least three times a week to collect someone . . . another Indian leaving Uganda. More than half the class was Indian, so now six rows had shrunk to three.

Coach wasn't even in yet, and Asha wondered if he'd make it to school. He had been at the house again last night, talking behind closed doors with Papa and Mr. Gupta. It was the third—no, fourth—night in a row she'd heard her teacher's worried voice as she walked down the hall to bed. When Asha asked Papa what they talked about all night, she always got the same answer. "Nothing you need to worry about."

But she did.

Clamoring at the door startled her and Asha looked up. Simon came into the room loaded down with his cricket gear. He jerked a hello with his chin before collapsing into the seat closest to the door. Leela followed, minus her sister.

"Leela," Asha called out. She waved to get her attention, but Leela hurried to her seat with her head bent and her chin tucked low. Only when she turned to pull out her chair did Asha see her red, puffy eyes. She rushed over. "What's wrong?"

Leela said nothing.

"Where's Neela?"

"She's not coming." Leela's eyes filled up and she shook her head.

Twenty-three days. That's what the announcer shouted this morning from the radio. They were running out of time, and with each day, more and more people were leaving. And now her friends were leaving too.

The morning bell rang and Asha returned to her desk. A group of kids fell through the door, laughing loudly. Yesofu wasn't one of them. She slumped back into her seat, listening to the classroom chatter buzzing around her.

"They had to leave their money in the bank . . . fifty shillings is all they're allowed to take."

"Can't drive anywhere . . . all the stations are out of petrol."

"Making us carry identity cards."

Asha missed when they used to gossip about the latest movie stars or fashions. As she looked around, she hardly recognized her classroom. Used pencils, opened textbooks, and bits of eraser lay scattered upon the many empty desks, almost as if the kids had gone out to recess or lunch. But Asha knew the truth. Nobody was returning to put their stuff away.

The second buzzer rang. Coach Edwin walked into the room. "Settle down!" he shouted, and clapped his hand against the desk for quiet. Asha's teacher looked like he'd rolled out of bed and come straight to school. His shirt—the same one as yesterday—had more creases than the crumpled paper on her desk and his hair lay matted on his head like a thick, black cap. Asha wondered how much of last night's conversations had to do with the way Coach looked this morning.

"We're continuing with chapter two. History of the East

African Railways." He picked up the textbook. "Let's start with . . ."

Asha flipped the pages in her text. What was it Simon had said? That their parents were working together against President Amin. Maybe they were helping people stay or helping them to leave. She glanced at Leela and thought about Mr. Gupta. His byline was almost always on the front page under the headlines, but it hadn't been there lately.

"Asha!" Coach Ewin called out.

Startled, Asha looked up. Everyone was looking at her. Coach pointed to the textbook. Asha cleared her throat and started reading. "The first large arrival of Indians to Uganda came with the building of the railroads at the turn of the twentieth century." Before she could continue, Simon's hand shot up.

"If we've been here so long, how come the president is kicking us out?"

"Because you Indians are trouble," Salim called out. Some African students snickered, but quickly stopped when Coach turned to look in their direction.

"It's what happened after the railway was built." Coach rested against the edge of his desk and explained how when the trade in Uganda boomed, the British turned to the Indians to run their businesses. "The British brought in Indians to work for them. Africans tried applying for jobs, but they were turned away."

"But that's not our fault," said Pran. He was in the same class as Yesofu and Asha. His father owned a large sugar plantation, and he often brought bunches of raw sugarcane to share at school. Asha looked at her bracelet and thought about how Yesofu hated the dried canes that cut his fingers and arms.

Simon nodded in agreement. "Pran's right."

"But it's not our fault either."

Suddenly Asha felt ice cold. She turned and saw Yesofu standing in the doorway, his backpack slung over his right shoulder.

"My dad works in the fields, so why can't he own a piece of the land? He's tried to buy land and banks wouldn't give him a loan."

Had Yesofu's dad always wanted a piece of land? How come she didn't know? A bunch of hands went up and questions ricocheted back and forth. *Why is Amin punishing us? Whose fault is it? Why are Indians being blamed? How come the British didn't hire Africans?* Coach clapped his hands.

"Take a seat." He pointed to Yesofu. "These are good questions, but the answers aren't simple. They are messy and tied to years of history in Uganda. There is no one person or group to blame. There is a lot that is unfair."

More hands shot up. The class waited, but it seemed Coach was done answering questions.

Yesofu kept his back to Asha as he slipped into one of the

remaining empty desks, right in front of her. She reached out her finger to poke him in the shoulder but changed her mind, quickly pulling back her hand.

"Yesofu," she whispered.

He didn't respond.

"Yesofu," she said, a little louder this time.

He leaned forward and rested his elbows on his desk. Asha slipped off her friendship bracelet and tucked it into the front pocket of her school uniform.

Coach started reading where Asha had left off, but paused at the sound of footsteps. The classroom door opened and the principal gestured for their teacher to step outside. The whole class stayed quiet. Leela's book fell to the floor. She looked at Asha. No. No. No. Asha wanted to jump up and lock the door behind Coach. Stop the principal from taking away anyone else. Stop him from taking Leela. The door opened. *Please don't be here for her. Please.*

Coach walked over to Leela. "Your uncle is here."

No. Asha twisted to get out of her seat, but froze when Coach shot her a warning glare. Leela's chair scraped against the floor. The sound pierced Asha's ears and she winced. Leela shuffled slowly, her head down. When she reached the door, she glanced over her shoulder. She looked at Asha and held her gaze before stepping outside. Tears pricked Asha's eyes and she clenched her fists. Her fingernails dug into her palm. She wasn't going to cry. Not at school. Through a small gap in the door, she saw Coach reach into his jacket and pull out a small, brown bundle, which he handed to Leela's uncle.

The door shut. Asha folded her arms on her desk and put her head down.

Leela and Neela gone.

Two more empty desks.

≫28≪

YESOFU

YESOFU KEPT HIS eyes on the clock, counting down the final seconds to the bell. After Leela left, he'd spent most of the afternoon sticking close to Yasid and avoiding the Indian kids' stares. Even Coach seemed distracted, teaching a lesson on fractions and then handing out a science paper. His mind was elsewhere and his eyes kept darting from the window to the door. Did it have something to do with the brown packet Yesofu had seen Coach give Leela's uncle?

Buzzzzzz!

A blast of hot air hit Yesofu as he burst outside. Playoffs were starting soon, but he'd have to miss practice today. There was no sign of Asha under the banyan tree, which meant she'd already started for home. Yesofu ran in the direction he

146

and Asha always walked. He pictured Akello throwing fruit at her, or worse, shoving her around. He ran faster, until his lungs felt like they were burning. At the top of the hill, he stopped. A group of four boys huddled together, blocking the road. Apart from Salim, Yesofu didn't recognize any of them. Like a herd of wildebeests, they moved toward Asha. The boys stopped a few feet away from Asha and then Akello stepped forward.

"No!" Yesofu shouted. He waved his arms, but nobody saw him, their attention focused on Asha. He saw her try and make a run for it by darting around them, but Akello blocked her path. Yesofu ran up behind her.

"These are friends of mine," said Akello. "And in case you're wondering, none of them are *shamba* boys. Isn't that right, Yesofu?"

Yesofu saw Asha flinch. She spun around and looked at him, her face full of questions and hurt. "You've got it all wrong," he said quickly.

Akello stared at Yesofu. "What are you talking about? I'm doing this for you."

"I'm not a part of this. You've got to believe me, Asha."

"After everything she's done and said, you show up here like *she's* your best friend."

Asha tuned back and faced Akello. "*Usinisumbue!*"

"Don't use our language." Akello grabbed her backpack. "You want me to leave you alone. Ask in English."

Asha snatched her bag back. *"Ninaweza kuzungumza Kiswahili."*

Swahili was her language too, and she'd told him as much. The boys with Akello laughed.

Yesofu looked back and forth between Asha and Akello. He didn't want anything to happen to Asha. But stopping them meant going against Akello. A flicker of orange and yellow caught his eye. Their friendship bracelet.

Yesofu faced Akello. "Let her go."

Akello ignored him and stepped forward, closing in on Asha. She moved away, but he reached out and grabbed her arm.

"Get off!" Asha yelled, and kicked him in the shin.

"Filthy *Mhindi* pig." Akello shoved her.

Asha fell backward, hitting her head on the hard dirt.

"Simama!" Yesofu shouted.

"Stay out of this, Yesofu," barked Akello.

"No! Leave her alone." Yesofu stood up to Akello.

"Why are you still protecting her?" Akello's voice was thick with hatred. He kicked a rock at Asha. "She thinks she's better than us."

Salim snickered. "So much better that she thinks she's too good to be a real Ugandan."

"I am Ugandan!" Asha yelled. "I was born in Entebbe. This is my home."

Akello seized Asha's arm and pulled her up. "You're

nothing but a filthy Indian," he said through clenched teeth. "You look down your nose at Yesofu and laugh at his dad." He shoved Asha and she fell into the scrub brush.

A boy Yesofu didn't know laughed and spat at her. Asha wiped her cheek and winced. She must be hurt.

"*Acha!*" Yesofu shouted for them to stop. He rushed to get to Asha, but Akello grabbed him, pinning his arms.

The same boy picked up a clod of dirt and threw it at Asha. Yesofu kicked and struggled to get away, but Akello held him tight in his grip.

"Leave me alone." Asha lifted her arms as another clump of reddish dirt hit her cheek. She clenched her fists. "Go away, please . . . *tafadhali.*" Asha's words came out as barely a whisper.

"Look at the Indian begging. . . . Please . . . *Tafadhali.*" Salim and Akello laughed.

Asha pulled her knees to her chest.

Yesofu's fists balled up. He couldn't stand it anymore. He wrenched free from Akello and punched him in the stomach. "You better leave her alone," he threatened.

Akello's eyes filled with rage. He socked Yesofu in the chest. "That's for being a traitor."

The punch knocked the wind out of Yesofu and he doubled over. Akello grabbed his shirt collar and pushed Yesofu down, pinning him against the ground.

"Get off me!" Yesofu struggled under the weight of Akello.

"I was there for you. We all were. And you still pick her."

"Stop!" A sharp voice broke into the hubbub. "Get off him."

It was Esi. He reached down and pulled Akello off Yesofu and held them apart. He glanced at Asha but made no move toward her. Asha uncurled and pushed herself up from the dusty ground. Smudges of reddish-black dirt covered her face. Bits of sand and gravel were matted in her braid. She brushed the dirt off her school uniform and picked up her backpack, holding it tightly against her chest like a shield against all of them. Even Yesofu.

"What's going on?" Esi asked.

"Akello and his . . . ," Yesofu started, but his voice was lost as everybody started talking at once—except Asha. Esi looked from Yesofu to Akello and then Asha.

"Go home," Esi told everyone.

"I'll go with Asha." Yesofu took a step forward.

"No." Asha stared at Yesofu. She turned and limped away.

Yesofu watched her shoulders moving up and down. He wanted to talk to her, but Esi had a firm grip on his arm.

Akello walked up to Yesofu and stared him hard in the eyes. "You don't deserve to be Ugandan." He spat on the ground and kept going.

29

ASHA

ASHA CLIMBED UNDER the covers and pulled the blanket to her chin. She'd told Mama and Papa she was tired, but really she couldn't stand the way they kept looking at her. She had a gash above her eye that Mama had treated. A crisscross of cuts and scrapes covered her legs, and she had red welts where Akello had grabbed her arm. The worst was her hip. A nasty bluish-black bruise, the size of her carrom striker, had started to form, and it throbbed.

Asha leaned over and picked up the photo frame on her nightstand. She and Yesofu stood on the banks of Lake Victoria with their arms around each other's shoulders, grinning into the camera. She didn't want to think what could have happened if he hadn't been there today. For a split second, she'd thought he was in on it with Akello, their way of getting back at her for calling them *shamba* boys. But then he'd stepped in to help her and she didn't know what to think. Asha laid her head back.

Fara peeked inside and smiled at Asha. "How's my *malaika*?"

Asha hugged the photograph against her chest. Fara sat on the edge of Asha's bed. Gently she removed the picture from Asha's hands.

"This is one of my favorites too." She set the frame back on the nightstand. "A lot has changed since that photo was taken." Fara took Asha's hand and clasped it between hers. "You and Yesofu have been good friends—"

"He's my best friend," Asha cut in.

"I know," said Fara. "But right now things are hard. Sometimes, *malaika*, you have to let go of the things precious to you. Some people know when to let go . . . others hold on too tightly."

At that moment Mama appeared, holding a bottle of iodine and a wad of cotton. "I need to disinfect your scratches again."

Fara got up. She brushed a loose piece of hair behind Asha's ear. "I am glad my boys were there today." Then she turned and nodded to Mama as she left.

Mama had undone her braid, and her thick, dark hair fell

in waves around her shoulders as she came to sit on the edge of the bed. Two small lines nestled just above her nose, in between her eyebrows. She unscrewed the lid on the bottle of medicine.

Asha pulled back the gauze. The gash on her leg looked worse. The skin around the cut was red and puffy. "Will it leave a scar?" she asked.

"It shouldn't," said Mama. She tipped the iodine bottle upside down. The white fluffy ball turned yellowish-brown as the medicine soaked into the cotton pad. A pungent, sharp smell burst into the air and Asha wrinkled her nose.

"Did you know that Leela and Neela were leaving?" Asha asked.

Mama nodded. "I didn't want the time you had left together to be filled with sadness." She paused for a minute and then continued. "You should know, Simon's family got their papers to leave."

"How soon?"

"In two days. They were accepted into the US."

Asha shut her eyes. All she could think about was how fast everything was changing.

"This will sting a little," said Mama as she dabbed the cotton ball on Asha's leg. She always said that when she applied iodine. Not that it ever made it hurt any less.

Ting. Ting. Ting. Mama's gold bangles jingled as her hand

moved in quick, gentle flicks. The iodine burned and Asha focused on the sting. It gave her something else to think about other than Akello and Yesofu and that all her friends were leaving. She felt Mama staring at her and opened her eyes.

"What?" Asha said, unable to keep the anxiousness out of her voice.

"I'm thankful you're safe." Mama pulled up the blanket and tucked it around Asha tightly. "None of this is your fault. You know that, don't you?"

A warm breeze blew into the bedroom and the curtains billowed. Asha nodded and felt her stomach tighten. "Then whose?" she asked. "Yesofu for being friends with Akello? Akello wanting to help his friend?" Then more softly, she added, "Me? For being friends with Yesofu and making fun of Akello?"

For a long while Mama didn't say anything. Her eyes filled with tears. "This shouldn't have happened to you. All I want is for you to be safe. For my family to be safe." Mama pressed her lips against Asha's forehead. Then she added softly, "Maybe your stubborn mama is to blame. For refusing to leave."

Asha glanced at the shelf behind Mama where the passports were hidden. She thought how she was just as stubborn. Maybe even more. Maybe that's what Fara meant by *holding on too tight*. Asha threw her arms around Mama's neck and squeezed, breathing in the familiar and comforting scent of sandalwood and coconut oil. They stayed together for a few minutes, holding one another. Then Mama kissed Asha on the forehead and shut off the lamp. The room went dark, but as the door clicked shut, Asha heard Mama whisper, "I love you, sweetie."

20 DAYS

≋30≋

YESOFU

YESOFU SHOVED HIS feet into his shoes, curling his toes as they pushed against the tip. Mamma and Baba were arguing about him and Asha again. You'd think they'd be tired of the same conversation. He was. It was hard not to hear Mamma and Baba. Hanging straw mats served as walls in their hut to separate the space into three sections. A main room for eating meals, cooking, and relaxing. A room for Mamma and Baba. Another room for him and Esi to share. His whole house could fit inside Asha's kitchen and sitting room. Yesofu glanced at his watch. School started in forty minutes and he still had to eat breakfast and grind the maize into flour for *ugali*—a grainy, doughlike bread made from cornmeal.

The second Yesofu stepped into the kitchen, Mamma

159

pointed to the wooden mortar on the ground and the three-foot wooden pestle leaning against the wall. Yesofu looked inside the wooden bowl. Kernels of dried maize covered the bottom. Breakfast would have to wait. He picked up the wooden pole and started crushing the small yellowish kernels.

"We've taught our son not to judge people by their skin color," Mamma said to Baba. "African or Indian. He could be friends with both."

Yesofu pounded the corn, wishing this conversation would end. He hated that he was the reason Mamma and Baba were arguing.

"That was okay before, but now . . . ," Baba said. "He's forgotten who he is, where he comes from."

Yesofu froze. Baba sounded just like Akello. They were wrong. Hanging out with Asha and Simon didn't make him less African. "I know where I come from," he blurted.

Baba's head snapped in Yesofu's direction. "You think you do. But you don't. This never would have happened if you just—"

"What?" said Mamma. "If he just hung out with Akello and Yasid? If he stood there and let Akello hurt Asha?"

"He wouldn't have had to step in to defend Asha against Akello." He stared at Yesofu, daring him to say something.

Thud. Thud. Thud. Yesofu banged the long stick against the side of the bowl. Baba didn't come right out and say it,

160

but Yesofu knew what he meant. He wanted him to stay away from Asha. Well, Yesofu wasn't going to.

"You're being unfair," said Mamma. "We taught our son to be a good person, and that includes being a good friend and helping not just Asha, but anyone when needed."

"Life is unfair," said Baba. "There's no telling what state our country will be in once the Indians are gone. Amin's soldiers are getting more forceful. Until then—"

"I know," said Mamma. Her voice quieted to barely a whisper. "Mrs. Gomez and I talked. She doesn't want Yesofu near Asha any more than I do."

Yesofu dropped the wooden pestle, catching the bowl of ground maize flour before it tipped over.

"Good," said Baba. "And you?"

"What about me?" Mamma asked.

"There's been talk about Mr. Gomez," said Baba. "And I don't want any trouble. Amin's soldiers are arresting anyone even suspected of working against Amin . . . Indian or African."

Yesofu wondered what Baba had heard. He'd thought it was strange when he'd bumped into Mr. Gomez at the Evergreen Grocers and Provisions Mart and he left without buying anything. But that didn't mean he was doing anything illegal. Did it? But if Baba was worried about Mamma, that meant Asha could also be in danger. He had to see her. It didn't matter what Mamma and Baba said. Yesofu glanced at the basket in the corner next to the metal water pails. He'd better add an offering to the ancestors, especially since he planned on disobeying Baba.

"I'm off to work while I still can. Jobs are getting harder with the Indians leaving." Baba came over to Yesofu and pulled him in for a quick hug. "*Ninakupenda.*"

Yesofu watched Baba leave.

"He means it," said Mamma. "He loves you." She took him by the shoulders and looked into his face. "Stay away from Asha." Mamma paused. "It's for your own safety. And hers."

Yesofu stared at Mamma. Her fingers dug into his shoulders like they were pleading with him. He had to say something, even if he didn't mean it. "Fine. I will."

31

ASHA

"ASHA!" PAPA SHOUTED. "Let's go."

From her bedroom, Asha heard the front door slam shut. She shoved her feet into her sandals and snatched her carrom striker off the nightstand. At Mama's insistence, she'd spent the past five days stuck in the house. No school. No meeting friends at the Entebbe Club. So, when Papa asked if she wanted to go into town with him this morning, of course she'd wanted to. She couldn't remember the last time she and Papa had spent time together. Phone calls, late night meetings . . . there wasn't any room for her. She'd make sure today was different—convince him to stop for a snack at Café Nile, and even a game of carrom.

"Bye," Asha called to Fara, and stepped outside without waiting for a response. The passenger door was open and Papa crouched against the seat, pulling papers out of the glove box.

"What are you doing?" she asked.

Papa stood, leaving the papers scattered on the seat and floor. "I'm looking for our passports. I can't find them anywhere. You haven't seen them . . . have you?"

"What?" Asha couldn't look at Papa. Her eyes would give her away. She stared at the open glove box and reached for the carrom striker in her pocket. "Passports. I don't know. Um . . . N-n-no. I haven't seen them. I don't have them . . . why would I?" *Shut up, Asha*, she said to herself. She stopped talking, the knot of lies gathering in her throat.

Papa ran a hand through his hair. "I don't know where they are. . . . Maybe I left them at the bank."

Asha tightened her fingers around the striker. She pictured the passports hidden inside her carrom bag and blinked faster, wondering why Papa wanted their passports now. There'd been no talk of them leaving. "Why do you want them?"

"Better to be safe," said Papa. "It's getting harder to get out. London is making trouble about taking us. . . . If we don't get our vouchers now, who knows where we'll end up."

So this trip with Papa wasn't about spending time together.

It was about him getting them out of Entebbe. Asha wondered if Mama knew. She sank into the seat. Good thing she'd taken their passports. They'd probably have left already if she hadn't hidden them.

Cars honked the closer they got to India Street. Papa stared straight ahead, gripping the steering wheel like it was about to fly off. A brown envelope lay tucked against his leg. Asha picked it up. It was tightly sealed—licked and taped— with no name or address. Her fingers traced the outline of something thin and hard inside. It felt like a small book— too small for a novel . . . but about the right size and shape of something familiar—a passport book. But if she had their passports, whose were these?

"Stop it," Papa said sharply. He snatched the envelope out of Asha's hands.

Asha slumped back against her seat. The blast of a car horn yanked her attention outside. Traffic clogged the street as cars and motorbikes changed lanes, fighting to enter the narrow entrance into the petrol station. A bicycle taxi swerved in front of them and Papa slammed on the car brakes. "We never had a gas shortage before . . ." His words trailed off, but Asha knew what he meant . . . he meant, before President Amin ordered the Indians to leave.

As Papa neared India Street, the traffic lessened and he parked the car beneath a cluster of overgrown eucalyptus trees. Before getting out, he tucked the package inside the inner pocket of his jacket. He opened the back door and the menthol-cool scent of the trees rushed inside. Asha stepped outside and breathed in the freshness, pushing aside the questions about the packet tucked inside Papa's pocket.

"Come on," said Papa. He took Asha's hand and tucked it inside the crook of his elbow. "First stop is Evergreen Grocers and Provisions Mart."

"Can we can stop for a snack at Café Nile?" Asha asked.

Papa remained silent. He stared ahead, searching the crowd like he was looking for someone. Asha clenched her jaw. She unhooked her arm from Papa's and followed him around the corner onto India Street. It looked familiar . . . the same shops, the same signs, but the shops lining the long narrow street were empty now—the windows broken. Asha stopped outside the Sari House, remembering the hours she'd spent inside watching Teelu try on *sari* after *sari*. They'd even planned a trip there for when she came home in a few weeks. It was her sister's favorite shop. Wait until she found out what had happened.

"Things are getting worse—aren't they?" Asha asked. She stared at Idi Amin watching her from the posters pasted on the shop windows and telephone poles.

Papa ran a hand through his hair. "I don't want you to worry."

Asha chewed the inside of her cheek. She and Yesofu

weren't talking. Papa was walking around with hidden passports. Black-booted soldiers teemed in the street.

Every second.

Every minute.

Asha's worry was growing.

32

YESOFU

YESOFU STARED AT Asha's empty chair. Five days later, and he still hadn't seen her. At least he knew where she was. Simon hadn't shown up one day, and only later he found out that he'd left. Yesofu wanted to know if Asha was okay, if she was coming back to school, but he couldn't ask Mamma, not when he'd promised that he'd stay away from her. A wet wad of paper struck Yesofu in the back of the head. He spun around. Two seats back in the next row, Salim laughed and stuck out his tongue.

"Yesofu." Coach walked over and tapped the desk. "Turn around."

Salim snickered. Yesofu folded his arms across his chest. The past five days had been torture. Now Yesofu felt like he didn't belong anywhere. Not with the kids from the neighborhood and definitely not with the couple of Indian players left on the cricket team.

"Everything stinks," Yesofu said to himself.

The lunch bell rang, and he crammed his books inside his desk.

"I want to see the cricket team on the field five minutes before lunch ends," said Coach.

The team was starting playoffs in two days. Yesofu needed to practice his bowling. Officers from secondary schools would be watching, and if he played well, he had a good shot at getting a scholarship. It'd be great if they offered him one for all four years, then he'd show Baba how cricket wasn't a waste of time.

By the time Yesofu got outside, all the lunch tables with African kids were totally filled.

Except one. It was bad enough having to put up with Salim in class, but now he'd have to sit with him too.

"Hey," Yasid shouted, waving.

Yesofu walked over and sat down.

Salim turned around. When he saw it was Yesofu, his eyes narrowed. "*Potea!* No room for traitors here."

"Leave him alone," said Yasid. Salim looked surprised, but kept quiet. Yesofu opened his tiffin. Mamma had packed vegetable stew and a piece of *ugali*.

"How's your girlfriend?" Salim asked.

Ignore him. Yesofu ripped off a piece of *ugali* and dunked it into the stew. *He's an idiot.*

"Did you make Asha feel better?"

Salim made gross kissing noises that sounded like snorting pigs. He punched the guy next to him and laughed like he'd just heard the funniest joke in the world. Yesofu's hands shook as he took another bite. His jaw moved faster and faster as he swallowed his anger.

"Shut up!" Yasid snapped.

"But—" Salim started.

"You're being a jerk."

Yesofu kept silent and watched Salim and Yasid stare at each other. Finally, Salim looked away.

"You're the jerk," muttered Salim. He got up and left.

Yasid turned to Yesofu. "Don't let him get to you."

Yesofu glanced at his watch. It was almost time to meet Coach. He sopped up the last bit of stew. With a lot of Indian players leaving, Coach had held some extra tryouts to add new players. Yesofu had convinced Yasid to try out. He was pretty good at batting from playing with Yesofu on their makeshift field at home, and he'd made the team.

Out on the field, a couple of team players had gathered. Yesofu and Yasid joined them.

Yesofu looked around. Where were the others? There couldn't only be five of them. Had that many Indian players

170

left since the last practice?

Coach blew his whistle. "I wanted to talk to the team about the upcoming playoffs. You guys have worked really hard to get ready, especially with all the changes."

Yesofu didn't like the way Coach was fidgeting with his whistle. He had a bad feeling.

"But the playoffs have strict rules and we've lost more than half our team . . ."

Yesofu curled his hands into tight fists.

"I'm sorry, guys; I pulled us out of the playoffs." Coach paused. "I had no choice."

No, they couldn't be done. Yesofu needed cricket. He needed this game. He got up and stepped forward. "But our team actually had a chance of winning this year."

"There is no team," Coach said. "We have five players." He stopped and looked at Pran, Samir, and John.

"What about holding more tryouts?" Yesofu asked.

Coach shook his head. "The deadline is getting closer . . . and by finals, we might all be gone, except for you and Yasid."

Yesofu couldn't give up. There had to be a way to get more players for their team.

"The bigger problem is the school," Coach added. "With so many teachers and students leaving, it might have to close."

Yesofu didn't want to hear any more. He grabbed his tiffin and took off.

"Wait!" Coach yelled after him.

Yesofu ignored him and kept running. He got on his bike and started pedaling.

President Amin's plan was supposed to help him—not ruin his life.

33

ASHA

ASHA HURRIED TO keep up with Papa as he wove through the crowd. Today wasn't turning out at all like she'd thought. She was with Papa, but his attention was only on the passports.

At Mr. Kapoor's shop, Papa pulled her inside. Asha blinked as her eyes adjusted to the dim light. The usual freshness that made her mouth water had been replaced by something else. A musty smell of empty rice sacks and the sweetness of overripe bananas hung in the air. Two African women with shopping baskets stood together and picked through a crate of cassava. Asha couldn't remember a time that she'd been in the shop and hadn't run into someone they knew.

The wooden floor creaked as Asha trailed Papa to the

counter. Instead of his usual smile, Mr. Kapoor stood looking anxiously toward the door. His medium-sized belly pushed against the front of his *kurta* and he puffed slow, shallow breaths. He nodded slightly at Papa and adjusted the turban on his head. The muscles in Papa's face twitched.

"Go get some mangos to take home," said Papa.

Asha'd seen half a case of mangos on the kitchen counter this morning. "But—" She swallowed her words as Papa stared at her with pleading eyes. "Okay," she said quietly.

"Thank you, sweetie." Papa turned and walked over to the counter.

"Hello, Ashok," said Mr. Kapoor. "I wasn't sure you'd make it."

Papa patted his pockets. "I have a list here somewhere . . . give me a minute."

While Papa rummaged and searched, Asha peered inside the wooden crates stacked along the side wall. She'd heard Fara complaining that the shops were empty, but this was bad. The shallow crates—usually brimming with mango, guava, and green bananas—contained barely enough fruit and vegetables to cover the bottoms. There was only one mango left. Asha pressed it, feeling the soft flesh move beneath the skin. Ew. Suddenly a shadow fell upon her.

She looked up.

A soldier carrying a baton stood outside.

Asha took a step back. He looked past her into the shop,

his eyes dark and menacing. Then he smacked his baton against the palm of his hand and continued walking until he passed out of her sight. Asha let out her breath, snatched the mango out of the crate, and hurried to the counter. Her fingernail pierced the soft flesh as she plopped it down on the wooden surface.

"Perfect choice," said Papa, and he reached inside his jacket.

Asha looked toward the window. There was no sign of the soldier. She heard the soft crinkling of paper and turned as Papa pulled out his package. He lifted the mango and slipped it underneath. Mr. Kapoor glanced at the two African women before snatching the mango and the package off the counter. Asha glanced at Papa, but his face was still and unyielding. Mr. Kapoor's stomach rose and fell with every breath.

Asha was sure the packet contained passports. And that meant Simon was right. Papa was working against President Amin to help people get out of Uganda. That was the *too dangerous* that Mama had talked about. And now with Simon's dad and Mr. Gupta both gone, that left only him and Coach. What was Papa thinking?

Mr. Kapoor put a paper bag on the counter and leaned closer to Papa. "I can't thank you enough, Ashok."

"Be safe, Sanjeev," whispered Papa.

Footsteps thumped up behind them and then suddenly

stopped. Papa placed his hands on Asha's shoulders and pulled her closer.

"Mr. Gomez, isn't it?"

Papa gripped her shoulders, as if in warning, and then let go and turned. "Something I can do for you, officer?" His voice was calm and steady.

Asha turned. The soldier had returned.

"You work for the ministry of tourism?" The soldier smacked his baton against the side of his leg. "Heard you've been busy down there."

Thwack. Thwack. Thwack.

Asha wondered what else the soldier had heard. Papa pulled her closer. From behind the counter, Mr. Kapoor's breath came in short puffs.

"Today I'm spending the day with my daughter." Papa picked the plastic bag off the counter. "If there's nothing else . . . I've got to get home."

Thwack. Thwack. Thwack.

The soldier stepped aside. Papa pushed Asha out the door and they started down India Street.

Passing by the empty shops, Asha counted all the things the soldier knew. Papa's name. Where he worked. That he was working late. It all meant one thing—Papa was being watched. She wanted to scream. When they'd reached a safe distance from Evergreen Grocers, Asha turned to him. "What was inside that package?"

"What package?" said Papa calmly, but the muscle in his jaw twitched like he was grinding a clove with his teeth.

"The one you gave Mr. Kapoor?"

"It's nothing." Papa glanced at Asha but moved steadily toward the car.

Papa was lying. Asha took a deep breath. "Are they passports?"

A look of alarm swept across Papa's face. He stopped and grabbed Asha. "Forget about that package," he said, leaning in closer. "Do you hear me?"

Asha nodded. Papa's fingers dug into the soft flesh under her arms and her eyes watered.

Slowly Papa loosened his grip. "It's better if you don't know everything. Do you understand?"

Asha frowned. She wasn't sure. She remembered how frightened she'd been when that soldier appeared in Mr. Kapoor's shop, glaring at her like he could see the thoughts in her head. What would she have said if he'd asked her about the package? What would have happened if she had revealed the truth? She looked at Papa, into his deep brown eyes, identical to her own.

"I d-d-don't want anything to happen to you."

Papa cupped Asha's chin in his hand, his palm warm with a slight scent of musk from his aftershave. "Mr. Kapoor needed my help. But that is all I am going to tell you. It will be okay." He took her hand and together they walked to the car. With each step, her thoughts pounded beats like the rhythm of African drums.

Mr. Kapoor.

Passports.

Soldiers.

34

YESOFU

THE RAINS LAST night had left the dirt path to the well rutted and muddy. Yesofu squeezed his toes tighter to stop from slipping as his feet sank into the ground. Back and forth every day, carrying buckets of water and collecting firewood. This couldn't be all he had to look forward to—spending hours under the hot sun chopping sugarcanes and then back home to his chores. He filled both buckets at the same time so he wouldn't have to make two trips. The muscles across his back and shoulders pulled and strained with the weight, and his arms felt like they were about to fall off.

Without cricket, there definitely wouldn't be a scholarship. And with everyone leaving, who knew how long it would be before the primary school closed.

Yesofu's foot slipped and water spilled out of the buckets onto his leg. He caught his balance and continued, slower this time.

"Want some help?"

Yesofu stopped and turned. Akello sat on top of the planks of wood covering the old well. Water dripped down his face and neck, but it wasn't enough to wash off the stubborn dust and bits of dried cane that coated field workers. It was the first time they'd talked since their fight. Yesofu found himself wanting to catch Akello up on everything going on at school, especially about their cricket team. But then he remembered how Akello had pinned him to the ground and bullied Asha. "From you? No thanks." He kept walking.

From behind, he heard Akello running to catch up. Yesofu fixed his gaze on the path ahead, focusing on making it to the bottom of the hill without falling on his bum.

"You're mad," said Akello. "I get it."

"No, you don't," Yesofu snapped. "What you did to Asha was wrong." Yesofu felt his anger reaching toward Akello. "You're a different person since . . ." He wanted to say, *Since your dad came back*. Instead he said, "Since you quit school. What's going on with you?"

Akello took a long while answering. "Baba's gone."

His words were low and heavy, like the buckets in Yesofu's hands. Yesofu couldn't tell if Akello was relieved or disappointed. "Is he coming back?"

Akello shook his head. "Probably better if he doesn't."

"What are you going to do?"

"Get a job somewhere and then—"

Yesofu saw his and Akello's plans disappearing with every word out of his mouth. "You're giving up."

Akello grasped Yesofu's shoulders, and water sloshed out of the buckets onto their arms and legs. "You think I don't still want to go to secondary school?" Akello burst out angrily. "I can't. I have no choice."

"Coach says everyone has a choice."

"Yeah, well, it's easy to say that when you don't have to worry about food. I don't want my sisters to go hungry." Akello took one of the buckets from Yesofu and they continued down the hill. He stopped when he got to their makeshift cricket field. "When do playoffs start?"

"We're out. The team only had five players left." Yesofu looked at the field they'd built. He couldn't remember the last him he, Akello, Yasid, and Salim had played.

Akello set down his bucket and picked up a ball. "Let's play."

"Now?"

"Why not? Unless you're ready to admit that Rajeev was the better player." Akello grinned as he tossed the ball up and down.

Yesofu put down his bucket and snatched the ball in midair. "You're on." He gripped the worn red cricket ball in his hand, feeling the thick seam against his palm. Akello stood at the crease, tapping the edge of his bat into the ground.

"You going to stand there stamping out ants or play?" Yesofu called out.

Akello looked up and faced him.

Yesofu tightened his grip on the ball and began his run-up. He raised his arm, and just as he was about to pitch, the sound of scrambling feet came up behind him.

"Boo!" shouted Namata and Sabiti—Akello's sisters. They were a couple of years younger than Yesofu, but they didn't go to school like Akello. Instead, they sold fruits and vegetables in town with their mamma to help earn money. Only they didn't make enough. Yesofu understood Akello wanting to help his family. He'd do the same if Mamma needed him.

"Get lost!" Akello yelled.

Namata put her hands on her hips and narrowed her eyes. "Mamma wants you home."

"Yeah," added Sabiti. "Now!"

Akello leapt up and growled. He raced toward them, waving his arms. Namata and Sabiti screamed and took off running with Akello right on their heels. He stopped when he reached Yesofu. "You and me . . . we okay?"

Yesofu nodded. "*Sawa sawa.*"

Outside, the shadows deepened. Since Amin, everything had been changing so quickly. No cricket, no playoffs, and soon, no school. His future was just getting harder to shape.

Yesofu picked up the two buckets of water and walked back to his hut.

What was he supposed to do?

35

ASHA

CRACK!

A sharp sound ripped Asha awake. Every nerve and muscle tingled as she pushed her covers aside. Confused, she looked around, taking in the flowing fabrics by the window and the paisley bedspread. Then she remembered coming to Teelu's bedroom in the middle of the night and crawling into her sister's bed. She'd hoped it would make her feel closer to Teelu, but she'd fallen asleep missing her more. Asha turned toward the window. Through the sheer curtains, moonlight poured into the bedroom. The night was quiet. It was probably a dream. Asha straightened the sheets and was about to lie down when the crunching of footsteps prickled her ears. The shadow of a head rushed past the window.

Someone was outside.

Asha fumbled to pull back the covers. Fingers trembling, she freed her legs from the twisted sheets and slipped out of bed. Slowly, she crept to the window and peered into the darkness. A crescent moon cast a faint glow across the garden. Asha squinted, trying to make sense of the shadows. A small white car sat behind Papa's Mercedes in the driveway. It looked vaguely familiar . . . white . . . a crooked antenna.

Mr. Gupta's car!

But Leela and Neela's family had left over a week ago. Two figures emerged from the side of the house and moved toward the car. One stood taller than the other. They stopped below the window and spoke in low voices: "forgot," "servants' quarters," "right back." Then the shorter figure darted in the direction he'd just come from. It had to be the person she and Yesofu had heard in the servants' quarters.

Bushes rustled and the shorter figure came back into view. Asha heard a soft click, and light from a flashlight swept across the garden. She immediately recognized Papa, but the other man . . .

"Shut it off!" called Papa.

Before the garden plunged back into darkness, the shorter person turned slightly toward the light. Mr. Gupta. Asha stumbled into the nightstand. Her hand hit the edge and the bedside lamp fell with a noisy clatter. How long had Mr. Gupta been hiding in the servants' shack? Was he there when the soldiers came looking for his sister? Or was it someone else hiding? Asha shuddered, remembering the soldier waving his gun around. If he'd known about the servants' quarters . . . if he'd found someone hiding there . . . she shut out the thought. Feet hurried down the corridor. The bedroom door opened and Mama appeared.

"What are you doing in here?"

"O-outside . . . it's Leela and Neela's dad," stammered Asha. She pointed out the window.

Mama crossed the room and shut the window, whipping the curtains closed. "Nobody is outside."

Asha shook her head. "I saw Papa—"

Mama turned. "He's fast asleep in bed and that's exactly where you should be."

Asha took a step toward the window. "But Mr. Gupta's car . . . it's there in the driveway."

Mama placed a hand on Asha's shoulders and led her back to her room. She pulled the covers up to Asha's chin, tucking the loose edges under the mattress, firm and tight. Her lips brushed Asha's forehead. "Close your eyes and sleep."

Asha waited for the door to shut before struggling to free her arms from the tight cocoon Mama had wrapped her inside.

What about our safety? Mama had said to Papa earlier that night. *We'll be fine staying as long as you don't get too involved.*

But Papa *was* involved, and it looked like it was more than just the passports. Asha wondered if Leela and Neela had known that Mr. Gupta wasn't leaving with them. Was that why Neela hadn't come to school? And why their uncle had picked Leela up instead of her dad?

Asha crawled out of bed and opened her wardrobe. She felt around for her leather carrom bag and pulled it out. The passports were still inside. When she'd taken them, she'd been sure that Prime Minister Heath in London would stop Idi Amin. And if he couldn't do it alone, then the president from America, Nixon, or Prime Minister Trudeau in Canada would help. But so far, nobody had been able to stop President Amin. Asha emptied the bag onto her bed. She picked up Papa's passport and looked at his photograph, remembering what he'd said to Mama.

Stop fooling yourself! We cannot hide the color of our skin, so we will not be safe.

7 DAYS

⋙36⋘
YESOFU

"THANKS, COACH." YESOFU couldn't believe that Coach had agreed to talk to the officers at Lake Victoria Primary School about him joining their cricket team midyear for the playoffs. He'd worried that Coach would say no. So, on his way over, Yesofu had come up with a bunch of reasons to convince him. But it turned out he didn't need them.

"You're a good all-rounder, but don't forget your studies," said Coach. "The primary exams will be coming up soon, and you have a real shot at a scholarship."

"I won't let you down," Yesofu said before leaving.

Things were looking up.

Asha lived a couple of doors from Coach, and Yesofu had to pass her house on his way home. As he got closer, Yesofu heard the door slam and saw Asha burst outside. She started slapping the bougainvillea with a rolled-up newspaper, then deflated, sinking into a wooden chair.

"Asha!" Yesofu didn't care what he'd promised Baba. He couldn't just walk away.

Her head jerked up and she wiped away tears with the back of her hand. Yesofu walked over, stopping at the bottom step leading onto the verandah.

"Why are you here?" Asha gave him a hard stare and threw the paper on the table.

Yesofu shifted his feet back and forth, weighing whether to stay or go. He walked over and slipped into the chair opposite her. "I didn't think Akello would hurt you. I would have stopped him before . . . well, everything."

Asha didn't say anything, but her fingers fiddled with the beads on the bracelet he'd given her. "Then how come it's taken you so long to come see me?"

"Okay." Yesofu stretched out his hand to grab the bracelet. "If we're not friends anymore, I guess I'd better take that back." He grinned, daring her to stop him. The sides of her mouth twitched, like she was trying hard not to smile.

"It's not Akello," said Asha.

"Then what?"

Asha smoothed out the newspaper. "It's Teelu. She can't come home."

"Does that mean you'll go to London?"

"I don't know." Asha slid the paper across the table. The headline read NO MORE ASIANS. The photograph showed people holding signs telling Asians to get out. "Papa said that London isn't taking any more Indians." Her voice cracked, but she continued. "Nobody wants us. The United Nations is begging other countries. It's like we're the plague, not people."

"Your dad works for the ministry of tourism. Can't he do something?"

"He's doing something, just not to help us."

"What do you mean?" Yesofu tried to ignore the uncomfortable feeling creeping up his spine.

"Well, last night . . ."

"And?" Yesofu nudged, wanting her to keep going.

Asha rolled the bracelet around her wrist, faster and faster. She took a breath and looked like she was about to talk, and then stopped like she was weighing if she could trust him. They'd never had secrets from one another. Finally, she looked up and continued.

"I think Papa was in the garden with Leela and Neela's dad—Mr. Gupta."

"Didn't he leave?"

Asha pressed her thumb against the faces in the newspaper, like she was trying to rub them out. "Papa's got passports."

Asha poked a hole and then another, leaving behind faceless bodies holding signs. "Not one or two . . . like a whole bunch of blank ones."

Yesofu's jaw tightened. "What's he doing with them?" His voice came out sharper than he'd meant.

Asha's hand froze. She looked up, her eyes wide. "I d-d-don't know." She looked away quickly.

"You must know something."

"I told you. I don't." Asha gave him a sideways look that told him she was worried. "It's probably nothing."

"It doesn't sound like nothing. Blank passports. Hiding people."

"Who said anything about hiding people?"

The air between them crackled. For several seconds neither of them spoke. Then Asha reached out and grabbed both his hands in hers.

"Forget what I said."

Yesofu felt his stomach pitch.

"Promise you won't say anything." Asha rolled her friendship bracelet off her wrist and placed it in Yesofu's hand. "Promise on this."

Yesofu looked at the bracelet and dropped it. "I've got to go."

Asha grabbed his hand. "You have to keep quiet . . . for Papa . . . for me."

Yesofu didn't want anything bad to happen to Mr.

Gomez. But if Asha's dad was doing something illegal, then he should be stopped. Taking passports from his job didn't sound okay. Yesofu remembered Dada Amin's speech at the cricket match about first the British taking what they wanted and then the Indians. That was exactly what Mr. Gomez was doing. Yesofu pulled his hand out of Asha's grip and got up, clumsily stepping back.

"I'll see you soon, and Asha . . ."

She looked at him, her eyes begging for a promise.

"I'm sorry about Teelu," he said instead, and left.

5 DAYS

≈37≈
ASHA

"WHAT IF YESOFU tells someone? What if he tells Akello?" With nobody to talk to since her friends had all left, Asha'd telephoned her sister.

"Well, he hasn't told anyone yet. And Yesofu is your friend," said Teelu. "He won't break his promise."

Asha sank to the floor, careful not to get her foot caught in the telephone cord. That was the problem. There was no promise. Yesofu had shot out of her garden like his feet were on fire. "I don't know, Teelu," she persisted. "That stuff about Papa and Mr. Gupta and—" Asha swallowed. "The passports."

"Stop worrying," said Teelu. "Even if Yesofu tells Akello . . . and I'm not saying he will . . . it's not like Papa is doing anything really bad. You know they would have put Mr. Gupta in jail for the stuff he was writing. Papa had to help him get out of Entebbe."

Asha heard a voice in the background. "One of the nurses is calling," said Teelu. "I'll try and ring you later."

"Wait. What should I do . . . Teelu . . . Hello . . . Teelu?" Asha stood and hung up the phone.

It was late afternoon and the house was quiet. Papa and Mama were at work. Fara stood in the garden clipping wet sheets to the clothesline. Asha could see her through the kitchen window. A pot simmered on the cooker. The aroma of cloves, cinnamon, and cardamom wrapped around Asha, and she breathed in the smell of *masala chai*. Usually warm and comforting, today the smell did nothing for her.

Was Teelu right? Was she worrying for no reason? Papa had taken her into town when he met Mr. Kapoor. She wasn't really supposed to know what he'd been doing that day, but Papa had trusted her to see the exchange. She couldn't stand it if her slip with Yesofu ended up getting Papa arrested. Asha slumped into a chair. She thought about the two passports hidden in her room and wondered if she should put them back in Papa's office. If they left like Papa wanted, then they'd all be safe and together, but that meant leaving her home and Yesofu. She didn't know what to do.

The telephone rang. Asha snatched up the phone. "Hello, Teelu?"

"Asha . . . is that you?"

"Hi, Coach."

"Asha. Go get your father."

"He's at the office," she mumbled, shocked by the sharpness in Coach's voice.

"What about your mother?"

"Nobody's home but me and Fara."

There was silence on the other end of the line. Had Coach hung up? Then she heard breathing, coming in short gasps, and finally Coach asked, "Did your father leave anything for me . . . um . . . a small package . . . an envelope?"

How did Coach know about the passports? She remembered that night when she saw Papa and Mr. Gupta in the garden. A third person had been standing by the car. Asha glanced at the hall table where the mail was kept. Two blue aerograms lay inside the silver tray. She lifted the tray up and looked underneath. "There's nothing here."

"Are you absolutely sure? It's really important." Coach sounded panicked. "Your father was supposed to meet me, but he didn't show up, and now . . . now I don't know what will happen . . ."

In the classroom, Coach never lost his cool, except for that one time with Akello. Asha had never heard him sound so desperate. "I can check Papa's office," she said. "It's where he keeps his important papers."

"Yes. Yes, good idea."

"Where are you? I—"

"The green house at the corner of Suna Road. But, Asha, get your dad . . . don't—"

Coach's voice broke off and the phone buzzed.

"Coach? Coach?"

Asha hung up the phone and shot a quick glance toward the kitchen. Pots banged and the kettle hissed. Asha's nerves tingled as she crept down the hall. She wasn't allowed in Papa's office when he wasn't home, but he was always telling her to use her head when making choices, and that's exactly what she was doing.

Thin slivers of light peeked through the heavy wooden shutters in Papa's office. She searched the desk, lifting the stacks of files and papers, hoping to spot the brown bundle or envelope. Nothing. Asha pulled open the drawers. Nothing. She shut the drawer and yanked open the heavy double drawer with all the files. Still nothing. Then she got an idea. She slid her hands down the side and under the files, stopping as her fingers wrapped around a tiny bundle. She pulled it out and stuffed the bundle in the pocket of her pants, pulling her tunic down to hide the slight bulge. Then she slipped quietly out of the study.

"Fara! I need to run an errand. I'll be right back!" Asha called out before running outside, past the white sheets flapping in the breeze toward Suna Road.

38

YESOFU

YESOFU WAS WAITING for Esi at Café Nile. He couldn't believe his brother was at the bank getting papers for a loan. It was almost enough to make up for Baba's trouble finding work since the Indians running the coffee and sugar fields had left.

"*Chakula kiko tayari!*"

Yesofu looked up.

"Your food is ready." Mr. Bhatt waved to him from behind the counter.

Yesofu had been surprised to see the café owner still here and wondered if he would be leaving. The deadline was in five days. Yesofu walked over and picked up the plate of *mhogo*, careful not to burn his fingers on the deep-fried cassava root.

"Where's your friend?" he asked.

Yesofu knew Mr. Bhatt was asking about Asha. Whenever Mamma sent Yesofu to buy supplies for Mrs. Gomez, Asha'd come with him and they'd stop at Café Nile.

"Has she left?" he asked.

Yesofu shook his head. "No."

He walked back to his table, wondering about Asha. It had been two days since she'd told him about Mr. Gomez and he was still trying to make sense of everything. Esi had been no help when Yesofu talked to him. His only advice had been to stay out of it. With Teelu stuck in London, Yesofu figured that Mr. Gomez would probably leave and then none of this passport stuff would matter. It wasn't like Asha's dad was actually doing something to hurt Dada Amin. He was helping Indians leave and that's what President Amin wanted. Yes. Keeping quiet was the right thing to do—especially for Asha. She'd never forgive him if something horrible happened to her dad. He could end up in Makindye—the headquarters of General Amin's military force. The word was, if you went in, you never came out.

Yesofu picked up a *mhogo* chip. "Ow!" He dropped it and blew on his burning fingertips. The door burst open and a group of soldiers walked in with some African boys.

Yesofu shifted in his chair, keeping his back toward the soldiers. He didn't trust them. Not anymore. Not after what he'd seen happen to that Indian man when he was last in town. And especially not after that soldier pulled out his gun at Asha's house. He'd heard the stories of people being arrested and shot, their bodies being dumped in Lake Victoria. He didn't want that happening to Mr. Gomez.

Keeping his head down, Yesofu touched another *mhogo* chip. Now it was cooler. He picked it up and popped it into his mouth. A shadow fell over the table.

"You're making me hungry!" Yesofu swallowed the piece of *mhogo* and then coughed as it went down the wrong way. He looked up, bracing himself to come face-to-face with one of the soldiers, and was surprised to see Akello.

Akello thumped him on the back and plopped down in the seat, laughing. "*Habari.*"

Yesofu took a sip of fizzy lemonade.

"*Utapenda kunywa nini?*" a server called out.

"Coca-Cola, *tafadhali,*" Akello answered. "You want anything?"

Yesofu shook his head.

"I saw you in Kampala this morning," Akello said.

"We'd gone to service." Yesofu popped a chip into his mouth. The family had taken the bus to Mengo Hill this morning to attend church at Namirembe Cathedral. Usually they attended service at a small hall in Entebbe, but today Baba wanted them to pray to God and thank him for the good things coming their way. Yesofu liked the big red tiled cathedral. The pastor didn't put him to sleep with a boring sermon like the one in Entebbe. He also felt closer to his ancestors. The *Kabaka*—the royal Buganda king—had given the land for the cathedral to be built.

"What were you doing there?" Yesofu asked.

Akello pulled a paper out of his pocket and spread it out on the table.

Yesofu leaned closer. "What's that?"

"Land for sale." Akello sat up straighter. "I've been saving from my jobs."

"Don't you want to use that money for secondary school and—"

"Look, we both know we're not going to school again. I can't and I'm pretty sure Norman Godinho will be closing soon."

"I'm joining Lake Victoria Primary. I'm gonna play on their cricket team and try for a scholarship."

"You're still gonna need money for fees, uniforms, and notebooks."

"Okay. So my plan's not perfect. I'm working on it."

The server walked over. "*Chakula kiko tayari!*" He set a plate of hot fried *mhogo* chips on the table. "I gave you extra to celebrate, but don't tell Mr. Bhatt."

"What's he talking about?" Yesofu asked when the server left. "What are you celebrating?"

Akello pointed to a grainy photo of a small house. "I found a place. But I need more money for the loan and if I don't come up with the rest quickly, someone else will buy it. It's perfect for us." He talked fast with excitement, the words spilling from his mouth. Yesofu hadn't seen him this happy in a while. He realized that it wasn't fair constantly going on at Akello about school.

"And . . . guess what?" Akello continued.

"What?"

"It has an acre of land and a real house, not like our place now. It'll have cement walls and rooms—one for Mamma, me, and another for my sisters. Maybe even . . ." Akello paused. "Are you ready?"

Yesofu nodded.

"Running water!"

Yesofu couldn't count the number of times he and Akello had wished for running water so they didn't have to make the trip to the well over and over again. "I've got news too," said Yesofu. "Baba wants to buy a shop. Esi went to get the loan papers."

"I told you the Indians leaving was a good thing. You get a shop. We get a farm. Go Dada Amin!" Akello popped a *mhogo* chip in his mouth. The soldiers at the counter turned and cheered with him. Akello waved.

Yesofu took a long sip of lemonade. It wasn't that he disagreed with Akello. President Amin was helping them. But was it fair that Simon, Leela, Neela, and Rajeev all had to leave?

"I heard that Britain doesn't want the Indians either." Akello laughed.

Yesofu remembered the article Asha had shown him. The angry white faces holding their signs of hate. Were Africans any different? They didn't want the Indians any more than the British did.

"Hey!" Akello tossed a chip at Yesofu. "Where'd you disappear to . . . dreaming of your shop?" He slurped the last of his Coca-Cola. "Five days. That's all the time left for Indians to get their visas and passports."

"I don't think that's a problem. The bank's not the only place for passports." Yesofu picked up a chip. His hand froze inches from his mouth. Oh no! What had he just said?

Akello's eyes got wide. "What are you talking about?"

"Nothing." Yesofu glanced at the counter . . . at the soldiers.

"Doesn't Asha's father work for the ministry of tourism?"

Yesofu saw a soldier look in their direction. "Shhhh! Just drop it."

Akello wouldn't. He leaned closer. "It's Mr. Gomez, isn't it? You should report him."

The soldiers got up. Akello lifted his arm like he was going to wave them over. Yesofu wasn't going to let that happen. He grabbed Akello's arm and pulled it down, holding it against the table until the last soldier left the café.

"I'm not going to do anything that gets Asha's dad in

trouble," said Yesofu. "Besides, I don't know anything for sure."

Akello didn't blink. "You may be fine with Indians always getting what they want . . . doing whatever they want. I'm not." He clamped the edge of the table, his hands shaking. "Asha has everything, living in that big house, going to private schools. But what about me?"

"This has nothing to do with you."

Akello stared at Yesofu. "It has everything to do with me. When is it my turn?" Akello yanked out of Yesofu's grip and took off.

"Wait!" Yesofu shouted. "What are you gonna do?"

≋39≋
ASHA

SWEAT TRICKLED DOWN Asha's back as she ran with the small bundle clutched in her hand. Her mind swarmed with so many questions. What if Coach wasn't there? What if there were soldiers on the street? What if she got caught? Her legs were starting to get tired, but she ignored the ache and kept running. She passed a couple of houses she recognized as belonging to families from the club, but nobody was out riding bikes, or walking, or sitting on their porches. Most of the houses seemed empty. Up ahead Asha saw the sign for Suna Road and ran faster. The green house was right on the corner. Asha stopped in the front yard and collapsed against the generous trunk of an umbrella tree to catch her breath.

The shutters in the front of the house were closed, tight

and unwelcoming. It didn't look like anyone was home. Asha unlatched the gate and stepped through. Should she knock or just walk in? Asha wrapped her hand around the doorknob and turned. It was unlocked. She pushed on the wooden door, just a little, and slipped through the opening, closing the door behind her. With the shutters closed in the late afternoon, the room was dark. She blinked as her eyes adjusted. White sheets covered the furniture and the shapes looked like shadowy crouching beasts in the dimness. She walked farther into the house and paused at the bottom of the stairs. Everything was silent.

"Coach?" Asha whispered, her voice vanishing into the quiet. "It's me, Asha." Her words bounced off the walls. Where was he? "Coach, are you here?"

A floorboard creaked above Asha's head. She froze. *Please be him.* She climbed the stairs, willing her feet to move one step at a time. She stopped briefly when she reached the top. Someone stepped out of the shadows.

"Coach." Asha stumbled over the top step in her rush toward him. "You're here. I came as fast as I could." Asha stopped to catch her breath. "I didn't see you outside and got worried."

"Did you bring it?"

"I found the package in Papa's office." Asha thrust her hand into her pocket. "Are you sure he won't be mad I took it?"

"I'm sure," said Coach. "Give it to me and then you better go."

"What about you?" asked Asha, running her finger over the papery edge of the package still in her pocket.

"I have to wait until—" Coach froze. Downstairs, something had slammed into the front door—once, then twice, then . . . Coach grabbed Asha and shoved her behind him as the door downstairs burst open and boots thundered down the hallway.

"We have to hide," said Coach.

Hide? Where could they hide? Any minute now the soldiers would swarm like angry hornets.

Downstairs, glass shattered. A voice bellowed, "Find him. Now!"

Panic flashed like lightning across Coach's face. He pulled open the door to the wardrobe in the corridor. On one side, towels and sheets lay on rows of shelves. On the other side, empty hangers hung from a small rod.

"Get in," said Coach.

Asha crawled through the narrow opening and scooted to the far corner. She looked back.

Coach put his finger to his lips, then shut the door.

Asha pressed her back against the wall of the cupboard. Through the tilted wooden slats in the door, Asha could see the corridor and landing at the top of the stairs. But not Coach. Where was he? A storm of boots thundered. Asha pulled her knees to her chest and wrapped her arms around them tightly. Two soldiers appeared at the top of the steps holding long, black batons. From all the stomping, she'd expected three . . . four . . . or even five soldiers—not two.

"Search every room," said the taller of the two soldiers. "He's here somewhere."

Batons banged. Boots thumped. Asha cringed. The noise hurt her ears and her heart beat fast and loud. So loud that she was afraid the soldiers would hear.

"I've got him." Through the slats, Asha saw a soldier with a big belly drag Coach out onto the landing.

"What are you doing here?" asked the skinny, tall one.

"This is my brother's house," said Coach. "I came to check on it. He's away."

Brother? Coach didn't have a brother. Asha stayed still.

"We know what you're really doing here," said the tall soldier, and he nodded. The big-bellied one raised his baton, bringing it down on Coach's shoulder with a crash that drove him to the floor. Asha gasped, and then pressed the heel of her hand against her mouth.

"President Amin knows exactly what you've been up to!" the tall soldier shouted.

"I d-d-don't know what you are talking about."

The big-bellied one grabbed Coach by the hair and pulled him to his knees. "Stop lying." He whipped his baton down upon Coach's head. Asha covered her head like she was the one being hit. She wished she had the courage to rush out there and stop them. The tall soldier brought the sole of his boot down on Coach's back. The force knocked Coach against the wall. He collapsed. Asha covered her face, but she couldn't block the sound of the blows or Coach's cries.

"No. Stop, *hapana*," Coach moaned.

"You're a conspirator and the president won't allow it."

Asha opened her eyes. The walls of the closet felt like they were closing in on her. Out in the hall, Coach was slumped against the wall, blood running down the side of his face.

"I d-d-don't know what you're talking about," he said. "I'm a teacher."

"Liar," said the tall soldier. "Kizza, what do we do with liars?"

The round soldier smirked. "We shoot them."

No! Don't shoot. Please. She shouldn't have answered the phone. She shouldn't have promised to help. Coach would have already been far away from this house. Kizza pulled out his gun. His hand trembled as he pointed it at Coach.

"What's going on up there?" a voice called out from downstairs.

"We've got him, sergeant," the tall soldier replied.

A burly soldier, bigger and scarier than the other two, appeared upstairs. He held a gun steady in his hands.

The sergeant looked at Coach slumped against the wall. "Who is this?"

The tall soldier straightened his shoulders. "Ashok Gomez, sir."

Was that who the soldiers were looking for—Papa?

"Idiots! This isn't him."

The tall soldier grabbed Coach's hair and pulled up his head. "Sir, look. It is him. He was in the house just like you said he would be."

"You've got it wrong. I'm Edwin. Edwin Patel. A teacher."

"Check his identification," said the sergeant.

Kizza put his gun away. He pulled Coach's wallet out of his pocket and searched through until he found the identity card. The sergeant snatched the card out of Kizza's hand. "It's not him. This guy's a teacher."

"Now what?" asked the tall soldier.

"Leave him," said the sergeant. "Let's go."

The two soldiers trailed behind the sergeant. Asha waited. Footsteps clomped downstairs. She gently pushed the door and peered into the corridor. Coach lay on the floor, curled in a heap. His hair was matted with blood and he had a gash on his cheek. She wanted to rush over and make sure he was okay, but not yet. She waited until she heard the sound of tires spinning in loose gravel. Then silence.

Asha got up, pins and needles poking at her feet and legs as she crawled out of the cupboard to where Coach lay sprawled at the top of the stairs. His right eye was swollen and he clutched his side, softly moaning. "Coach . . . it's Asha. Are

215

you okay? Can you walk?" She linked her arm inside her teacher's arm and tried to pull him up, but he slumped to the ground.

"No," he said through clenched teeth. His voice barely above a whisper. "Get out of here. Go warn your papa."

"No." Asha shook her head. "I can't leave you here."

Coach dragged himself to the banister and used the railing to pull himself up. His left leg hung—bent and twisted. He clenched his jaw tightly. With a sigh, he leaned against her, and she faltered under the weight. They started down the stairs and he stumbled. Asha felt his breath come in short painful gasps against her shoulder. He slumped to the ground and lay on the steps.

"I can't." Coach's face cringed with pain.

Coach was right. She'd have to go without him. "I'll get help." Asha took one last look at Coach before hurrying down the stairs.

Ashok Gomez. That's what the soldier said. She had to warn Papa.

≈40≈
YESOFU

YESOFU BALANCED ON the back of Esi's motorbike, clutching a bag full of spinach, potatoes, and cassava root for Mamma. Esi had shown up right after Akello took off. Yesofu hadn't said anything about what happened, especially since Esi'd told him to stay out of it. Good thing they were on their way to Asha's house. Yesofu needed to find out more about Mr. Gomez and the passports before Akello did something stupid—like talking to Amin's soldiers.

"Can't you go any faster?" Yesofu asked.

"Nope." Esi wove between the jumble of cars and bikes crammed on the road, rolling to a stop when he couldn't move any farther. "It's the deadline. Everyone's on the road."

Yesofu replayed his conversation with Akello in his head.

The bank's not the only place for passports. That's what he'd said. Akello had no proof that Mr. Gomez was doing anything illegal. Who'd believe him? Yesofu glanced at the soldiers standing on the street with their rifles clutched to their chests. The soldiers would want proof—wouldn't they?

Shouts came from up ahead on the road. Another checkpoint. With the deadline so close, stops were now everywhere. Two soldiers stepped into the traffic and started walking toward them. Yesofu clutched the bag of fruit and vegetables against his chest with one arm and held on to Esi with the other. The soldier reached for something on his belt. Yesofu saw a gun and shivered, remembering the day at Asha's house. He felt Esi tense.

The soldier pulled out a long, black baton and stopped at the white car up ahead. Ropes tied down a stack of suitcases to the roof. Another Indian family on their way out. The soldier motioned for the Indian man to get out of his car.

"What are they doing?" Yesofu whispered.

"Shhhh." Esi waved his hand to silence him.

Another soldier started pulling the suitcases off the roof. The husband fired off words, clipped and angry. The soldier with the baton spun around and hit the man in the head. The man staggered backward, clutching his head. Blood spurted from his nose. Esi made a move to get off the bike, but Yesofu pulled him back, not wanting anything to happen to his brother.

The soldier with the baton looked up. "*Enda!*" He waved his arm. "Go!"

The traffic started moving and Esi moved with it, slowly passing the white car. Yesofu shut his eyes. What if the man with the blood spurting from his nose had been Asha's father?

Yesofu had to find Akello. He couldn't be responsible for anything happening to Mr. Gomez.

"You okay?"

Yesofu leaned over his brother's shoulder. "*Poa*," he lied.

Esi finally turned onto the road leading to the hospitals. They passed the Grade B hospital, used by the locals. Up ahead at the top of the sloped hill was the Grade A hospital where Mrs. Gomez worked. Asha's house wasn't too far away. The Grade A hospital—a small, whitewashed one-story building sat across from the health ministry. It was used by wealthy Africans, like President Amin. Yesofu had been to the Grade A hospital with Asha a few times to visit her mom, but Sister Masani, who managed the ward, always gave him the stink eye from behind her desk—wealthy Africans only.

Yesofu squinted. Someone in a bright orange *salwar kameez* was running up the hill toward the hospital. Asha. "Let me off. Stop!"

Esi pulled the bike behind a truck, and Yesofu jumped off.

"What's wrong?" Esi asked.

Yesofu didn't respond. He saw Asha run around to the back of the hospital and took off after her. In the back, steps led to a wide verandah that attached to six patient rooms. The ambulance was parked in the courtyard.

"Mama! Mama!" It was Asha. Her voice rattled the doors.

Yesofu pushed open the glass door and darted inside.

Sister Masani had a hold of Asha's arm, but that didn't stop her from grabbing Yesofu. His shopping bag dropped, sending vegetables flying.

"Shhh! Why are you screeching like monkeys? You'll disturb the patients."

Asha yanked her arm out of Sister Masani's grip. "Where's Mama? Is she still here?"

"She's with a patient."

"You don't understand." Asha's voice crept upward, getting louder and louder. "I have to see her. Now." Asha started down the corridor. "Mama!"

Yesofu had never seen Asha like this before, her breath coming out in short, explosive bursts. And those reddish-brown splotches all over the front of her tunic, they looked like—blood. He swallowed. Yesofu tried to wrench his arm free, but Sister Masani's fingers tightened around his wrist.

"What's going on?" Mrs. Gomez stepped out of the first patient room and stopped when she saw Asha. She hurried to her side. "What's wrong?"

"It's Coach." Asha struggled to speak. "The soldiers beat him . . . called him a conspirator. He needs your help."

The picture of the man with blood running down his face flashed in Yesofu's head. Sister Masani's eyes darted back and forth between Mrs. Gomez and Asha.

"Nonsense." Mrs. Gomez shot Asha a warning glance. "Why would soldiers beat Edwin? He's your teacher."

"B-b-but . . . ," sputtered Asha.

Mrs. Gomez put up her hand to silence Asha. Then she turned to Sister Masani. "I'm heading home. The patients should be good for the night, but ring if you need me."

Yesofu stared at Mrs. Gomez. He could hear the fear in her voice, her words quivering and shrill. Sister Masani nodded. She let go of Yesofu and picked up her pen, making notes in a patient's chart.

Mrs. Gomez looked at Yesofu and seemed surprised to see him, like she'd just realized he was standing there. She put an arm around his shoulder and pushed Asha and him out the back entrance. "I have to get my bag. Meet me around the front on the verandah steps."

"What about the vegetables?"

"Sister Masani will take care of them."

Outside, Yesofu reached for Asha's hand. She didn't look at him, but her fingers clasped around his as they ran to the front of the hospital. The verandah was empty and all the doors leading to the patient rooms shut. Through the screen door, Yesofu stared into the dimly lit hallway. There was no sign of Mrs. Gomez. How long did it take to get a bag? He felt Asha's hand slip out of his.

"What happened?" Yesofu asked.

Asha looked away. "It was awful—"

He put his arm around her and she trembled. "It's okay." As the words came out of his mouth, he knew it was a lie.

Asha shook her head. "They beat him, Yesofu. They hurt him really bad."

"Why would they do that?"

Before Asha could answer, the doors swung open and Mrs. Gomez burst out, still in her white coat—but with no bag. Her eyes darted back and forth between him and Asha. She pointed to the steps. "Wait here. Your mamma is on her way to get you." Then she grabbed Asha's hand and led her away. "Come on. We better hurry."

The hospital ambulance, lights flashing and siren blaring, sped past. When Yesofu looked back, Asha and Mrs. Gomez had reached the bottom of the hill.

What didn't Mrs. Gomez want them to know?

41

ASHA

"SUNA ROAD IS the other way," Asha said. "Where are you going?"

"Home."

Asha stopped. "What about Coach?"

"Don't worry about him," Mama replied. "I arranged for an ambulance to take him to the hospital and Papa is contacting his parents."

Her bag was just an excuse. "You telephoned Papa, didn't you?"

The bun at the back of Mama's head bobbed up and down as she nodded. "What did he say when you told him?" Asha asked, and she hurried to catch up.

"Forget Papa. I want to know what you were doing."

Asha tried to figure out exactly how much to confess—sneaking into Papa's office, taking the package, lying to Fara. But with the next breath, she remembered the look of fear in Coach's eyes and the blood spurting from his mouth. This wasn't like the usual fibs she and Yesofu told. This was different. Dangerous. Scary. She met Mama's stern gaze and told her everything.

Mama stopped and held out her hand. "Give me the package."

Asha removed it from her pocket. She readied herself for the yelling to start, but Mama's mouth was sewn as tight as a rice bag.

As Mama and Asha stepped onto the verandah, the door flew open. Papa stood in the doorway. Mama thrust the package at him and then continued straight to the kitchen.

"Where did you get this?" Papa asked.

"Our daughter had it. She decided to help you by taking it to Edwin. When I think of what could have happened . . ." Mama's words were strangled and she pulled Asha into a tight embrace. "My brave girl. My brave, reckless girl."

"What about Coach?" Asha asked.

"I reached his parents," said Papa. "They're meeting him at the hospital."

Mama shook her head at Papa. "You promised our family would be safe," she said. "That nobody would get hurt. Now look. Look what could have happened to Asha."

"No," said Asha. Mama had it all wrong. "Papa had no idea I took the package."

Papa ran his hand over his tired face and looked out the window. "Your mother is right. I should never have brought those papers home. But Mira, you are the one who wanted to stay. And we stayed. Now you are blaming me for helping people, our friends. I can't stand by and do nothing while Amin is arresting and killing people. If I can help, I must. You said you understood." His voice was low and calm. He looked at Mama, his eyes pleading. "I love my family. I would never let anything happen to you."

Mama shook her head worriedly. She pulled Asha into the circle of her arms, pressing her close. Papa moved toward them, wrapping his arms around his family. Together like this, Asha felt as though nothing could hurt them. But she knew that wasn't true.

Mama's lips trembled, but she tried to smile. "I don't want anything to happen to you," she said, looking into Papa's eyes. Her hands clenched the front of her *sari*, wringing it between her fingers.

Asha stepped back, and she saw the package lying in the middle of the table.

"Papa, what's inside the package?"

Papa's lips pressed together, then he sighed. "Passports," he said. "They're for a man who worked with Benedicto Kiwanuka."

Asha shifted uncomfortably. Benedicto Kiwanuka, the minister of justice, had been dragged out of his courtroom by Amin's soldiers and taken to Makindye Prison. It was one of the last news articles Mr. Gupta had written. "Wasn't he killed?"

"Which is why I am helping this man get out of Uganda," said Papa. "I was supposed to meet Coach at the house on Suna Road and give him the passports, but soldiers were parked outside the office. I couldn't risk them following me, and I had no way to warn him."

"Now what?" asked Mama. "Will this man be all right?"

Papa picked up the passports. "Not without these. I have to take them to him."

"Ashok." Mama's eyes filled with panic. "The soldiers are looking for you."

Papa slipped the passports into his pocket. "I made a promise."

"You made a promise to us too."

Asha thought of the solider ready to shoot, only stopping when he learned that Coach wasn't Papa. "Don't go. Please."

Papa slowly uncurled Asha's fingers. He kissed her gently on the forehead and then turned to leave.

"I love you, Papa," Asha whispered, but he'd already gone.

42

YESOFU

MAMMA STOOD NEXT to Yesofu at the bus stop, muttering. Gathering her words, ready to explode like a thundercloud.

"We told you to stay away from Asha," Mamma said as they waited for the bus. "The two of you get together, and there's always trouble. Soldiers. Fights. When are you going to see that it isn't safe? Entebbe has changed. The two of you can't just roam around together. It's not good for either of you!"

Yesofu had never seen Mamma looking so frantic. Arms flying. Braids shaking. She had it all wrong. "We weren't together. I saw her running and she—"

Mamma put up her hand to silence him. "I don't want to hear it."

It was probably better if he kept his mouth shut. Otherwise he'd also have to explain how he'd visited Asha the other day. In this mood, Mamma would never understand. Only when the bus arrived did she break her silence.

"Get off at Lake Victoria. Baba is waiting for you."

Yesofu took a step forward and was pulled back as Mamma wrapped him into a tight hug. "*Sawa sawa*. Go now."

When Yesofu reached the lake, he saw Baba at the pier sitting in one of the small, wooden fishing boats. He waved and ran over.

"Get in," Baba said.

Yesofu climbed inside, moving the fishing rods to sit. He pushed the boat away from the pier while Baba reached back and pulled the starter cord. Puffs of smoke rose from behind the engine as the smell of gasoline looped around them. Slowly they backed away and started moving out toward deeper waters. Yesofu wondered how much Mamma had told him.

With the shore a distance away, Baba cut the motor. He pulled out a worm from a small tub and handed it to Yesofu to hook onto the fishing line. "Mamma couldn't say much on the phone, but she said something happened to your coach."

The hair prickled on the back of Yesofu's neck. He nodded.

"You know what a conspirator is?" Baba asked.

Yesofu dropped the worm. "No, sir."

"It's someone who's plotting against someone else by doing

the opposite of what they want or interfering with what they want. Idi Amin is arresting anyone he thinks is conspiring against him. Indians. Africans. Makes no difference." Papa cast his line. "Disagree with Amin and that's enough for him to call in his army."

Yesofu shifted and the boat rocked. "Is that what happened to Coach?"

Baba took Yesofu's line, hooked on the worm, and handed it back to him. "I don't know about Coach. But look what happened to that judge. He was dragged out of his courtroom for disagreeing with Amin and taken to Makindye." Baba snapped his fingers. "Poof. He's gone . . . disappeared."

Yesofu thought about Mr. Gomez. If word got out about whatever Asha's dad was doing . . . if Akello told . . . would soldiers come for him like they'd come for the judge and Coach? "Asha told me Mr. Gomez is—"

"He should have left when he had the chance," Baba cut off Yesofu. "Instead he's stayed and is risking his life to help other Indians. Africans too." Baba raised his arms and sent the line out. "Dangerous business. Not only for him. His family too."

Yesofu looked at Baba, sorting out how to tell him about Akello. Baba would be able to stop him from going to the soldiers. "I saw Akello at Café Nile today and—"

"Get the net!" Baba cried out. His line pulled tight.

Yesofu reeled in his line and tossed his rod inside the boat.

He grabbed the net, keeping his eye out for whatever was bending Baba's line into a U. It had to be a big one . . . maybe a king fish. The more Baba tugged, the more his rod curved. As he reeled it in, the boat pulled toward the shoreline.

"My line's stuck." In the muddy waters along the shore, something floated. Baba blinked. "I'm going to check it out. Stay here."

Yesofu watched Baba wade closer until he was a few feet from the shore. Something long was tangled in the weeds and elephant grasses along the shoreline. Even from where he sat in the boat, Yesofu could tell it wasn't a fish. Baba stopped and leaned in. Then, in a rush, he started toward the boat, splashing and fighting his way through the shallow water.

"What is it?" Yesofu asked.

Baba climbed inside and started the boat. He pushed the lever to full speed. The engine sputtered and smoked as Baba steered them away. The boat rocked and Yesofu grabbed the sides. What didn't Baba want him to see? He turned to look over the back. A body, all puffy and bloated, bobbed on the surface. A body in a suit and tie. Yesofu's stomach clenched.

Coach.

Mr. Gomez.

Asha.

The names crashed in his head. He had to stop Akello.

43

ASHA

ASHA PLACED HER hand on the receiver, but didn't pick up the ringing phone. The last time she'd answered, it had been Coach.

It rang again, for the fifth time.

Asha gripped the receiver tighter, but still she didn't answer. Whoever was on the other end wasn't giving up. Maybe it was Teelu? But what if it wasn't? Maybe someone was calling because Papa had been arrested. Maybe it was Papa and he needed help?

Asha lifted the phone and put it to her ear. "Hello?"

"What took you so long . . . Are you okay?" It was Mama ringing from the hospital. She'd finally agreed to let Asha stay home while she went back to the hospital to check on her patients.

"Sorry, Mama. Yes."

"Listen. A patient's gone into labor, so I won't be home for a while." She paused and then asked, "Is Papa back?"

"No."

There was silence at the other end of the line, but Asha could feel her fears as if she'd spoken them loudly. "Okay. I'll be home as soon as I can."

Asha hung up and ran back up the stairs. She wanted to stay in her bedroom. It felt safe inside these four walls. Familiar. She emptied the carrom bag onto her bed and picked up the passports. The lie she'd told Papa when he asked her about them stuck in her throat like a thorn. It was time to tell the truth. She'd give them to Papa and tell him that she'd been wrong to make them stay.

The clock ticked.

Seconds. Minutes. Hours.

Outside, the sun lowered and the sky changed colors, matching the beads in Asha's bracelet. Papa still wasn't home. Asha glanced at the clock on her night table. It had already been three hours since Mama'd telephoned. It was fine. Papa would be home soon.

Click.

Asha sat up. Someone was playing carrom. She climbed out of bed and tiptoed down the dimly lit corridor out the front door, onto the verandah. In her hand, she held the carrom bag with their passports. It was time to tell Papa the truth. Outside, ribbons of red and orange rippled across the sky.

Click.

The striker knocked a game piece into a corner pocket. The sound rang in Asha's ears.

Papa. He was home, sitting in the chair where he always sat when they played carrom, safe.

"Want to play?" Papa asked. He reached for the container of boric powder and sprinkled a light dusting of it on the board—just enough to make sure the pieces slid smoothly.

Without a word, Asha slipped into the chair opposite him. His cheeks crinkled as he smiled and reached across to brush the hair out of her eyes.

"Coach Edwin's going to be all right," said Papa.

A lump gathered in Asha's throat, relief and sadness intertwined inside her.

"You break," said Papa, and he passed her his championship carrom striker.

Asha set the disc on the baseline, positioned her fingers, and flicked the striker.

Snap! The collection of tan-and-black discs scattered across the wooden game board.

Two discs dropped into one of the four corner pockets. The remaining ones swirled across the board.

"Well done," said Papa. He leaned back and waited for Asha to take her next shot. "You did a brave thing today, taking the passports to Edwin."

Asha's hand shook and she missed, sending her piece flying to the opposite side of the board. She handed Papa the striker and watched him in the dim light. She thought about his smile, the way his face lit up when he saw her. How his hugs felt sure and strong. Her heart pinched in her chest and she took a breath. She couldn't imagine a day without him. "Before Simon left, he told me that President Amin has a list of enemies." She glanced up at her father, then back down to the board. "Are you on it?"

"It looks that way." Papa reached across the board and took Asha's hand. "But you'll be all right. You're my brave girl."

Asha glanced at the carrom bag. She'd taken the passports to help Mama, to help Papa see they didn't have to leave. No, she'd hidden them to help herself. To make sure she didn't have to leave her home. She looked at Papa. "I have to tell you something . . ."

Papa nodded at the board. "Let's finish our game."

Asha picked up the carrom bag. "But . . ."

"Tomorrow," said Papa. "It can wait."

Asha dropped the bag, relieved. She worried how Papa would react when she told him what she'd done. He'd be angry. No. Furious. She didn't want to ruin this moment. Papa was home. He was safe.

Click. Papa knocked another piece into a corner pocket. He smiled and placed the striker on her shooting line. Asha pushed down her worries. Tomorrow she'd give him the passports. It wasn't like he could do anything with them right now. The offices were all shut. For tonight she just wanted to play carrom. In the still of the night, just the two of them, it felt like nothing had changed . . . that Coach hadn't been beaten. That Teelu was still coming home. And that Papa wasn't wanted by Amin's soldiers. Asha wished she could hold on to this moment forever.

They played until the corner pockets bulged from the weight of the discs and only the striker remained on the board. Asha'd won tonight, but she wondered if Papa'd gone easy on her. He always won.

"I'm going to wait up for Mama," Papa said. "You better get to bed."

Asha walked around and hugged Papa, breathing in the woodiness of his aftershave. "You are also very brave."

He held her close. "Remember, sweetie," he said softly. "You have what everyone wants. You have love. Mama loves you. Teelu loves you. I love you. And as long as you have that, you have everything."

Asha lay in her room staring up at the ceiling. Tomorrow. First thing in the morning she'd tell Papa everything. She snuggled deeper under the covers. Teelu was stuck in London. School was closing because there weren't enough teachers and students. She had no idea if she'd ever see Leela, Neela, and Simon again. And Yesofu. Asha picked up her bracelet off her nightstand. Her Entebbe had almost entirely disappeared. Eventually, Asha rolled over and fell asleep.

Someone banged on a drum, the sound far away. With a start, Asha woke. She blinked, trying to see through the darkness. She raised herself up on her elbows. Everything looked the same, exactly where it should be. She listened, and slowly her shoulders relaxed. Asha pulled up the covers and lay back down.

"Open up!" a gruff voice shouted, followed by a loud knock.

A pale glint of light peeked through the crack in Asha's curtains. The banging started again, louder.

"Open up! Now!"

Not again. Not here. The soldiers couldn't come back for Papa. She wouldn't let them.

"Open up!" a brutal voice snarled, followed by more banging.

Asha slipped out of bed, turned the doorknob, and peered into the corridor. She saw Mama's dressing gown billowing behind her as she rushed down the stairs. Mama turned on the light at the bottom of the steps and glanced up.

"Back inside!" Mama ordered, then hurried to the door.

Asha couldn't be alone. She ran to Teelu's room, remembering at the last minute that her sister was in London. She shut the door and climbed onto the bed. She pulled up her sister's bedspread, imagining Teelu was here, wrapping her arms around her tightly. Only it didn't help. There was no way to block the soldiers' shouts.

"We're here for Ashok Gomez."

"Find him."

"Check upstairs. Look everywhere."

The sound of heavy feet stormed and thundered inside the house. Asha gathered the covers to her chin, cringing at the crash of boots coming from downstairs. The house shuddered, as if the walls were being bashed in. The floorboards creaked and cracked under the stampeding soldiers. Asha pulled her knees to her chest and wrapped her arms around her legs.

Angry voices crashed through the house.

"He's here somewhere."

"We're going to get him."

Boots clomped closer and closer and then stopped. Asha listened, her body trembling. Papa was smart. He'd helped Mr. Gupta and Mr. Kapoor. He'd find a way to get out of this. He had to. The bedroom handle jiggled and the door swung open, flooding the room with light from the corridor. A soldier, frightening and huge, loomed in the doorway with his baton ready to strike. His eyes glided toward the bed. Asha's breath caught in her throat.

The soldier remained frozen in the doorway. He fixed his

gaze on Asha, staring at her in silence. His hands loosened their grip on the baton.

Asha remembered Papa's words. *You're my brave girl.* She met the soldier's gaze.

"Don't hurt me."

"I'm not here for you."

She swallowed and leaned forward. "Please don't take him."

"I have to," he said.

"P-p-please—" Asha stammered.

The soldier's fingers tightened and loosened around his baton, like he was unsure.

"What will I do without him?"

"*Nasikitika.* I'm sorry."

"Please," Asha said, and then repeated herself, this time in Swahili. "*Tafadhali.*" The soldier's face slipped, and Asha thought she saw something behind his eyes. Then he blinked, and it went away.

≋44≋
YESOFU

YESOFU PULLED THE handle and water poured out of the spout into the metal bucket. He'd looked for Akello when he and Baba got home, but still couldn't find him. As shadows grew out of the well, he couldn't shake the feeling of dread, that he was too late. That Akello had done something that neither of them could undo. The image of the body floating in the lake was seared in his head.

As Yesofu reached the bottom of the hill, he heard footsteps coming toward him. Salim and Yasid appeared.

"Hurry! Come quick," said Salim.

Yasid was right behind him. "You've got to see this."

"What's going on?" Yesofu asked.

"Meet us at Akello's." Salim took off with Yasid right on his heels.

Yesofu set the water pails down right where he'd stopped and ran after Salim. *Please don't let it be too late.* He had to make sure Akello hadn't said anything. Outside Akello's hut, a crowd had gathered. Yesofu had a bad feeling.

Akello's little sister ran over and grabbed Yesofu's hand. "Come see what my brother got." She pulled him inside the small hut. "Look!"

In the middle of the room was a brown, plastic-cased, sixteen-inch, black-and-white television set. It looked exactly like the one Asha had in her house, except that it was connected to a humming portable electric generator. Salim and his twin brothers, Wemusa and Wasswa, sat inches away from it, digging their elbows into each other, jockeying to sit nearer. President Amin's face filled the whole screen.

"I'm sitting next to the president." Salim pressed his head against the television.

Wemusa pushed him out of the way. "I'm touching his nose."

Yesofu couldn't take his eyes off the screen. One of these would have cost around nine hundred shillings or more.

"So, what do you think?"

The voice came from behind and Yesofu jumped. He turned and saw Akello.

"Where—" Yesofu's words caught in his throat. He

swallowed. "Where'd you get it?"

"It was a gift." Akello smiled.

No one just gave gifts like that, and it wasn't even close to Akello's birthday. "For what?"

"A job well done," Akello said.

Yesofu couldn't shake the feeling that Akello wasn't telling him everything. Had he gone to Amin's soldiers with what Yesofu had told him? Was that who'd given him the television . . . to thank him? Was that the job?

"Can we talk?"

Akello pushed past Yesofu and stepped outside.

"That stuff I told you. About the passports?" Yesofu needed to be sure Akello hadn't told anyone. He couldn't be responsible. Especially not if anything had happened to Asha's dad. "It wasn't for sure. You didn't . . . go to the police, did you? Because, you know, it was just a stupid rumor."

"You calling me stupid?"

"What? N-n-no," Yesofu sputtered. "I just meant I don't want you to get in trouble for telling the soldiers wrong stuff."

"You don't have to worry." Akello pulled Yesofu into a headlock. "I'm not in any trouble." His breath was hot on Yesofu's face. "I thought about what you said and asked myself, what would Dada Amin do? And then I did it."

Yesofu wrestled to get free. "The soldiers . . . is that who gave you the TV? If you told, I'm going to—"

"What?" Akello twisted Yesofu's arm behind his back and

shoved him. "What are you going to do?"

Yesofu spun around and wrenched free. He stared Akello down. From behind he heard rumbling. A Land Rover with two camouflage-clad soldiers pulled up outside Akello's hut.

"Get inside!" one of the soldiers shouted.

Yesofu didn't wait to see Akello climbing into the jeep.

He was too late.

≥ 45 ≤

ASHA

ASHA GLARED AT the soldier.

"I have my orders," he said.

"Over here!" a voice called out from another part of the house.

The soldier standing glanced over his shoulder toward Mama and Papa's bedroom. He looked back at Asha, then walked away. From downstairs, Asha heard Mama's cries. A jumble of voices and shouting rose up. Asha thought she heard Papa, but she couldn't be sure. She scrambled off the bed and ran into the corridor. Soldiers stomped down the stairs and then it grew quieter.

Slowly Asha crept down the stairs and inched closer to the

front door. She stepped outside and crossed her arms, pressing them tightly against her chest. Cold air blew through her thin cotton *kurta* pajamas. Where were Mama and Papa? She saw two soldiers standing in the driveway, leaning against their rifles. The gate into the garden hung open, dangling off its hinges. Parked in the street were three military jeeps and a smaller white car.

"He's done nothing wrong. You can't take him!"

Mama. Asha spun around. A thin soldier gripped Papa with one hand while pushing Mama back with his other hand. He stared at Mama with open hostility, his eyes cold. The soldier yanked Papa's arm and began dragging him to the gate. Mama lunged forward. Her fingers gripped the thin cotton collar of Papa's tunic. "No!" she screamed.

"Go back in the house," said Papa. He spoke calmly as he held Mama's hands, placing them at her sides. "I will be fine, but Asha needs you . . . both girls will need you."

The soldier jerked Papa forward. "Enough!"

Mama fell to her knees, sobbing; her shoulders shook and her body trembled. The soldier shoved Papa toward the car. No! They couldn't take him away. Asha raced across the garden. She had to get to Papa. She scrambled through the gate, running to get to the white car.

"Wait!" Asha shouted.

The soldier holding Papa looked at Asha and then turned

his head in the opposite direction. Asha followed his gaze and saw the big soldier who'd pushed his way into the house. He crossed the street coughing and spitting into the road. The one with the cold eyes stopped, still gripping Papa's shoulder. Asha rushed forward and threw her arms around Papa, holding him tightly.

"What's going to happen?"

He looked down at her as she tilted her head up. "I'll be okay . . . and so will you."

"Let's go!" said Cold Eyes, his hand on Papa's arm.

Papa set his solid, steady gaze on Asha, and she saw a strength and determination that Amin's men would never break. He cupped her face, his palm warm and clammy. His fingers carried the faint scent of boric powder from the carrom game they'd played earlier. "I love you, sweetie," he said before getting into the car.

"I love you too, Papa."

Tires crunched as the car moved forward and drove off. One by one the soldiers climbed into their jeeps and followed. Across the street, a soldier flicked his cigarette into the bushes and climbed into his jeep. He turned and spoke to someone sitting in the passenger seat. As the jeep did a U-turn, the person looked out, a satisfied smile turning up the corners of his mouth.

Akello.

Asha bit down on her lip until it hurt. Was he the one who led the soldiers to Papa? Asha stood at the edge of the driveway, staring into the empty road where only seconds ago, she'd stood with Papa.

This was her fault.

4 DAYS

≋46≋
YESOFU

"WHAT'S TAKING THEM so long?" Yesofu asked again.

Mamma sat cross-legged on a mat, a bowl of dried *nambale* beans in her lap. She picked out the bits of stones and dirt, leaving the broken or chipped beans. "They have to be careful. We'll hear something soon."

Baba and Esi had gone into town to see if there was any news about Mr. Gomez. Yesofu hovered in the doorway, playing out all the possible scenarios in his head. Just because Akello had told the soldiers about the passports didn't mean that they'd arrest Mr. Gomez. What was Mamma always telling him . . . *Naye abasatu babisattula.* A secret is better kept by two than three. He should have kept his mouth shut. Maybe they'd let Mr. Gomez go if he promised to leave

Entebbe. *Please let that be what happened.* Yesofu's guilt sat on both of his shoulders—all that he had done and could not undo.

The announcer on Radio Uganda was talking about the foreign minister. Yesofu turned up the dial on the transistor radio and listened.

"Wanume Kibedi announced that Asian non-citizens who do not leave by the deadline will be rounded up and kept in camps. Idi Amin's soldiers continue to arrest people known to be working against the president and urges Africans to come forth if they have information."

And they will be rewarded with big TVs. Yesofu got up and switched the radio off. Outside, he saw Baba and Esi, walking through a crowd of cheering villagers, and he ran to them.

"What'd you find out?" Yesofu asked. Baba silently placed a hand on his shoulder, leading him back inside.

"Mr. Gomez's been arrested."

No. Yesofu felt every muscle in his body tense. And what about Asha? The bowl in Mamma's lap fell, spilling beans onto the ground. Baba walked over and helped Mamma into a chair.

"You suspected something was going on for a while now," Baba said to Mamma.

Yesofu crouched on the floor and started picking up the beans. Did Baba and Mamma know about the packages . . . about Mr. Gupta? But they hadn't told on Asha's dad. Was it because they didn't want to get involved or because what Mr. Gomez was doing wasn't really illegal? Yesofu put the bowl on the table and sat with Esi, Mamma, and Baba. Mamma reached over and wrapped her fingers around his hair.

"What is going to happen to Mrs. Gomez and Asha?" she asked Baba.

Baba shook his head somberly. "From what I heard, they're at home . . . for now."

"How did the soldiers find out?"

Yesofu knew the answer even before Mamma asked the question. He didn't move, his breath trapped inside him.

"Akello," said Esi. He shot a quick glance at Yesofu. "He was there."

"What does Akello have to do with any of this?" Mamma looked at Yesofu. "Do you know?"

Yesofu swallowed hard. "This is all my fault."

Everyone was silent, staring at him. Waiting.

"Talk!" Baba said.

At last Yesofu found the voice to tell them everything. "If I'd kept my mouth shut, then Mr. Gomez would be home with Asha instead of—"

"There's no way to know what part Akello played in Mr. Gomez being arrested," said Baba. "The soldiers were already suspicious. But you're right. You shouldn't have got involved. We told you to stay away from Asha and you didn't listen."

Mamma reached for Yesofu's hand. "I know it's been

difficult." Mamma squeezed his fingers. "Asha . . . she's been a good friend . . . but it's time to let her go."

Yesofu clenched his fists, fighting the knot in his chest. He didn't know how to let go. Or if he was ready to say goodbye.

"I am sure Mrs. Gomez will take Asha and leave before the deadline." Baba looked at Yesofu. "Stay away from her . . . do you hear me?"

"*Sawa sawa*," said Yesofu.

"I mean it, Yesofu." Baba went back outside.

Yesofu picked up a long bean pod and pressed his fingernail against the edge. What Mr. Gomez was doing was wrong, but he was doing it to help people . . . save lives? He squeezed, and a green bean slipped out of the pod. Mamma said it was time to let Asha go. Maybe that meant helping her see that it was time to leave Entebbe. He probably should have done it sooner. But first he had to tell her the truth.

≈47≈

ASHA

ASHA STOOD OUTSIDE Papa's office, feeling the weight of the passports inside the carrom bag. There'd been no word about Papa, but friends had promised Mama they'd contact her as soon as they learned anything. Mama sat at his desk, dumping out drawers and searching through papers. She had an appointment at the immigration office to get travel vouchers. London. Canada. Australia. United States. Asha had no idea where they'd end up. With the deadline in four days, whatever country would take them . . . that's where she and Mama would go. Asha removed the passports from the bag and walked into the office.

"Where could they have disappeared to?" Mama muttered.

Asha clutched the two passports in her hand, their

accusations of guilt burning into her palm. She took a deep breath and gathered her courage.

"Mama."

"Where are they?" Mama pushed her hair off her worried brow. She pulled out a thick file, sifting through the papers.

Asha's hands began to sweat. She gripped the booklets tighter, trying to find the courage but not knowing where to start. "It's my fault Papa got arrested."

Mama dropped the papers in her hand and looked up. "What do you mean?"

"Papa wanted us to leave Entebbe. You didn't want to go. Neither did I." Asha placed the passports on the desk. "That day after Papa went to apply for our travel vouchers, I found the passports and hid them in my room."

Mama stared, saying nothing. Was she disappointed or angry? Asha couldn't tell. The silence was unbearable, so she continued. It was better to get it all out. "That day Papa and I went into town, he was looking for the passports and I lied. If I'd given them to him, then we would have left and the soldiers wouldn't have taken him away." Asha sank into the chair. "I'm so sorry, Mama."

"It's not your fault." She pulled Asha up and wrapped her arms around her. "He could have got us passports like he'd done for others. If anything, I'm to blame for refusing to listen to Papa and leave when he wanted."

Asha buried her head in Mama's neck.

With the passports in her bag, Mama set off for the immigration office. She was determined they leave in the next day or two. Asha couldn't imagine actually leaving, but she knew they had to. She watched the clock. Eight. Nine. Ten minutes. Mama was far enough from the house. Asha went outside and hopped on her bike.

"Where are you going?"

It was the African boy who had moved into Uma Auntie's house next door. He was only about four, and every time Asha saw him, she was surprised. His was the first African family to live in her neighborhood. But it wouldn't be *her* neighborhood for much longer. Asha showed him her bracelet and told him that she was going to see her best friend. Then she started the four-mile ride to Yesofu's house. She had to see him. Say goodbye.

As Asha neared Katabi—the rural area where Yesofu lived—thorny scrub brush replaced fragrant frangipani trees. At the rounded hilltop, Asha stopped and caught her breath. Tin shanties stretched out like rows of dominoes, mixed in with clay huts. Up close the shanties were only a little bigger than her bedroom. A jumble of plywood, planks, and tin, they looked more like the play forts she and Yesofu used to build than homes where people lived. It was strange that he'd never told her about his home. But then, she'd never asked, and she should have. It made sense why he desperately wanted that scholarship for secondary school. He wanted to make a different life for himself.

As Asha pedaled into the maze of shacks, she heard laughter and saw three teenagers bent over large tubs, washing clothes. She'd ask them where Yesofu lived. Asha pedaled over and rang her bicycle bell. The three girls, their arms in the grayish water up to their elbows, stopped and stared at her.

"*Toka hapa!*" one of them shouted. "Go away!" She scooped some water into her palm and flung it at Asha. The murky, cold water hit Asha in the chin and trickled down her neck. Yuck! She recoiled with disgust. The other two girls laughed and then also started flinging water. Asha whipped her bike around. Her foot slipped on the pedal just as another handful of water hit her. Maybe this wasn't such a good idea. She didn't know where Yesofu lived or even if he was home. Up ahead, two young boys, barefoot and in shorts, chased after a soccer ball.

Asha pedaled up to them. "*Mambo,*" she greeted them. One of the boys darted behind the flapping sheets hanging on a clothing line. The other boy picked up the worn soccer ball and clutched it tightly, as if he was afraid that Asha would snatch it. She thought she recognized him from a lower class at school, but couldn't be sure. "I need your help," she said. "Esi and Yesofu." Asha thought she saw a quick flicker of recognition in the boy's eyes. "Do you know them . . . *unawajua?*"

The boy nodded and pointed farther down the road.

"*Ondoka hapa!*" a loud voice shouted behind Asha.

The boy's eyes widened and he ran away. Asha looked over her shoulder. Akello stood outside one of the shacks, balancing a wooden rod across his shoulders. On either end hung two metal buckets. He lifted the rod over his head and lowered the buckets to the ground. Water sloshed and spilled onto the red dirt around his feet. His eyes never left Asha's face. "You don't belong here."

Asha wanted to scream at Akello for what he'd done to Papa, but fear held the words and they burned her throat. Clutching the handlebars, she started pedaling in the direction the boy had pointed. She heard Akello's feet coming up from behind and leaned forward, pedaling faster.

Suddenly a rock hit the bike. The wheel jammed. Asha tumbled over the handlebars and landed on her knees, scraping her skin against the rocky dirt. She got up and faced Akello.

"You need to leave." Akello's lips curled. "You're just making things worse."

Asha took a step back. She looked down in the direction of Yesofu's house, where the boy had pointed. She really wanted to see Yesofu, but not if it would cause problems for him with Akello. She remembered Fara telling her that some people know when it's time to let go . . . others hold on too tightly. Asha had thought Fara was talking about holding on to life in Entebbe. But maybe Asha needed to let go of both Yesofu and Entebbe. She looked Akello right in the eye. "You're right. I don't belong here anymore."

Akello seemed surprised at first, but then a slow smirk spread across his face. Asha didn't care. Akello may think he'd won, but he was wrong. Someone in Katabi would tell Yesofu she'd been here. He'd know she'd come to see him and that she still cared. She picked up her bike and rolled it forward.

"I'm leaving," she said, and brushed past him.

"Not soon enough for me." He spat the words at her.

Asha dropped her bike. She spun around and shoved Akello hard. Startled, he stumbled and fell. Asha turned and broke into a run. Behind her, Akello's feet beat against the ground. She darted between two huts and hid behind large sheets hanging from a clothesline. *Don't let him see me.*

"I know you're here somewhere!" he called out.

She spotted big metal tubs near a cluster of eucalyptus trees. They were big enough for her to hide under, but she had to hurry. Akello was getting closer. Asha ran.

"There you are, you filthy Indian," shouted Akello.

No, he wouldn't catch her. A broad plank of wood lay in her path. She jumped onto it to widen the distance between them.

CRACK!

Her right foot broke through the thin wooden board and she fell.

Down. Down. Down. Nothing beneath her feet but air. Her arms knocked against the rocky sides and her bracelet snapped.

She hit the ground hard.

Everything went black.

48

YESOFU

YESOFU HAD SKIPPED school today at Lake Victoria Primary so he could see Asha. He turned the corner onto her road and pedaled faster. Nearly all the houses had signs in front. FOR SALE. Windows and doors were boarded up. He continued around the hedge of oleander, up Asha's driveway. He hopped off his bike and ran to the door. He lifted his hand to knock and hesitated, trying to work out what to say. He'd have to just come right out and tell her what happened, how he'd told Akello. She wouldn't understand, but he owed her the truth.

Yesofu took a deep breath and knocked. He waited. Nobody answered. Yesofu knocked again, this time a little louder. He counted the seconds in his head . . . one . . . two . . . three.

He got to ten and there was still no answer. Where was she? Yesofu heard scuffling. An African boy, maybe four or five, stood at the end of Asha's driveway. It was strange seeing him in this neighborhood. But with the Indians leaving, Amin's soldiers had started taking the vacant houses and moving in. "Have you seen the girl who lives here?"

The boy stepped closer. "She took off on her bike."

"Do you know where?"

The boy nodded. "To see her friend. She showed me her bracelet."

Asha had never been to Katabi before. Not once in the entire time they'd been friends. He always spent time in her world. Not the other way around. But today, she was coming to see him, and he wanted to be there to show her his house and the makeshift cricket field. His thoughts screeched to a stop. What if Akello was home? What if he saw Asha? Yesofu climbed onto his bike, his heart racing even before he set off.

No. No. No. Please don't let Akello be there. Yesofu pedaled faster, his world spinning as fast as the chain on his bike. The army roadblocks had increased but they only stopped Indians, waving the Africans to continue through. Yesofu pedaled through the roadblocks, avoiding eye contact with the soldiers.

He had to get home before Akello found Asha.

⇒49⇐

ASHA

ASHA WOKE TO the coldness of the hard ground seeping through her tunic. Her ribs throbbed. Her head pounded. She lay still and took short, quick breaths. A circle of light glowed at the top of the well and bits of torn cloud raced across a hazy deep blue. From the colors in the sky, she guessed it was close to six or seven. Mama would be back from Kampala with the travel papers, wondering where she was. But the last place that Mama'd ever think to look would be Katabi.

Asha rolled onto her side and sat up. She felt dizzy. Not the whirling, wobbly kind when you spin around too fast, but the kind that sends the sky swooping beneath your feet, making everything upside down. She collapsed against the rounded rock wall and lay there for a few minutes, waiting for the dizziness to pass. She tried again and slowly got to her feet. Her fingers traced the holes and crevices on the surrounding walls. Some were just big enough to use as steps. She dug her foot into one of the hollows, and then another. As her eyes adjusted to the dark, she kept moving, slowly inching upward. She kicked at the wall to find a place for her foot. There wasn't any. This was as far as she could climb. Asha's heart pounded and her knees wobbled. "Help!"

The rock wobbled beneath her fingers. Asha lunged to grab a thick root sticking out of the wall. *Snap.* She fell. *Craaack!* Her shoulder slammed into the bottom of the pit. She gasped to catch a breath, wincing from the pain. As she lay on the ground, she wondered if it had been a mistake coming here. No. She needed to see Yesofu. *Ting.* She strained her ears and listened. *Ting. Ting.* Her bicycle bell. A rock was jammed inside so when you pulled the lever with your finger the bell made a sharp clang. She'd know that sound anywhere.

Ting. Ting. Ting.

She heard feet scuffing far above, and then voices. Her heart thumped faster, giving her the strength to sit up. She leaned against the wall. Muffled voices became louder and clearer until they sounded like they were directly on top of her. Asha wrapped her arm around her aching ribs, took a deep breath, and lifted her head toward the light. "Help!" Her voice echoed in the dark. She heard scuffling and then two heads appeared. "Get Yesofu or Esi!"

Another voice in the distance shouted . . . an older voice. Fara? No, it sounded deeper. Esi? Feet clapped against the hard ground. The voice was closer now.

"Go. Get out of here!" Akello shouted.

Asha shrank back against the wall of the well.

"There's someone down there," said one of the boys.

"Get lost." Akello's voice had an edge to it. "You don't know what you're talking about."

Panic rose in Asha like waves.

"We saw her," the boys said in unison.

"You calling me a liar?" Akello said, daring them to challenge him.

"But she'll . . ."

Die. Asha finished the sentence for him. She'd die. She'd never see Mama, Papa, or Teelu again. And what about Yesofu . . . Asha remembered Papa's words. *You're my brave girl.* She straightened, breathing through the pain in her ribs. "You know I'm down here!" she shouted. "Get Yesofu!"

"Shut up!" threatened Akello. "Or I'll cover the well opening."

"Help!" Asha screamed.

Bang! A tin sheet slammed over the opening, plunging Asha into darkness. She slid to the ground. Her heart pounded so hard, each beat hurt.

≈50≈
YESOFU

YESOFU WENT TO the makeshift cricket pitch to throw the ball around. He needed to clear his head, but it didn't work—he kept looking at the road, hoping to spot Asha. Where was she? Maybe she got tired of waiting and left. The thing was, if she'd ridden home, they'd have passed each other. There was only one road into Katabi. It didn't make sense. Yesofu wrapped his fingers around the ball and pulled back his arm.

Ting. Ting.

Yesofu froze. Where did he know that from?

Ting. Ting. Ting.

No. He strained his ears and listened.

Ting. Ting.

It was louder this time. Yesofu felt his insides buzz with the same feeling he got when he unleashed the perfect spin on a ball. It was the bell on Asha's bike. A rock had jammed inside so the lever stuck halfway when you pulled it with your finger.

Ting. Ting. Ting.

Yesofu took off running. "Asha!" He ran up the hill and skidded to a stop. Then he spotted a bike lying next to the old well. Wemusa and his friends stood nearby. Yesofu picked up the bike and pulled the lever on the bell. *Ting. Ting.* Definitely Asha's. He could still see the broken end of the stick jammed inside from when they'd tried to poke out the rock.

"Wemusa!" Yesofu called out. "Where'd you get this bike?"

"It's your friend's. She left it when Akello started chasing her."

"What's going on?" Akello approached. His eyes locked onto Asha's bike and then slowly, like a cobra slithering, they shifted onto Yesofu.

Yesofu felt the fight coursing through his veins. "Where is she?"

Akello's voice lowered to a threat. "Who?"

"You know who. Asha." Yesofu lunged and tackled Akello to the ground.

"Get off me," snarled Akello.

266

"What have you done to her?" Yesofu punched Akello in the jaw. He and Akello struggled on the ground, slamming their fists into one another, rolling in a cloud of red dust. Suddenly Salim and Yasid were there, pulling him and Akello apart.

"Stop." Yasid looked back and forth between Yesofu and Akello. "What's going on?"

"H-h-he's done s-s-something to Asha." Yesofu gasped for air. His ribs hurt so much it was hard to talk and breathe at the same time.

Akello wiped the blood on his mouth with the back of his hand. "I have no idea what he's talking about."

"Liar!" Yesofu swung at Akello, but Yasid held him back. "You better not have hurt her or—"

"Or what?" Akello growled. He spat in the dirt, turned, and walked away with Salim.

Yasid put his hand on Yesofu's shoulder, but he shook him off. "What if we can't find her? I have no idea where she is . . ."

Yesofu. His name was barely more than a whisper. "Shhhh. Did you hear that?"

Yasid nodded. "Where's it coming from?"

Yesofu.

"The well!" they both said at the same time.

Yesofu reached the old well first. The planks usually

covering the opening were broken and tossed to the side. Someone had dragged a tin sheet and covered the opening. With Yasid's help, Yesofu pulled it off and looked down. He squinted as his eyes adjusted to the darkness. Then he saw her.

"Asha!"

≋51≋
ASHA

ASHA SAT UP, unsure if what she was hearing was real. The tin sheet covering the opening of the well moved and was gradually pulled off. A trickle of pebbles and dirt skittered down. Asha looked up. The sky had blurred from deep blue to midnight black, and the stars, tiny pinpricks of light, covered the sky.

"*Mambo.* Are you there?" a muffled voice hissed into the darkness.

"Yes." Asha looked up, searching the narrow shaft. She saw a figure over the edge of the well, silhouetted by the moon. "Yesofu?" Her voice shook with relief.

"Yes. *Sawa?*"

"I'm okay," she said. "My arm hurts. And my side."

"I'm going to get help," said Yesofu. "It's late. Mamma and Baba should be home."

"No!" Asha cried. "I don't want to be alone again."

"I have to," said Yesofu.

The sound of his voice was the first bit of hope she'd had in hours. "Please."

"I'll be back. I promise."

"Wait!" Asha called out. "I'm sorry for everything. I've been selfish . . . only worried about myself. I'm sorry for never asking about you. For never coming here before today. Really sorry."

Feet pounded, moving away, gradually growing quieter and quieter. Yesofu had gone. Asha was alone again, with only the sounds of the cicadas for company. The moon had turned the deep, dark sides of the well into crags of shadows and light. She lifted her head and gasped as pain—like a knife jabbing her—shot through her body. She dropped back against the ground. *Hold on, Asha.* The edges of the moon blurred, growing smaller and smaller like a kaleidoscope closing, and then there was nothing.

"Over here!" a voice called.

There was clanking and rustling as hurried feet approached.

"I've got the torch and ropes."

"Baba has gone to Asha's house."

Asha knew these voices. Yesofu, back like he'd promised. And he'd brought Esi and Fara with him. A head appeared at the top of the well, and suddenly the dark pit came to life with a yellowish glow. "What's happening?"

"We're going to get you out," Yesofu called. "Esi is climbing down."

"Be careful," said Fara. "She could have a concussion or broken bones."

Asha's entire body shivered with pain, but her shoulder was the worst. *Keep your eyes on Esi. He's here now. Everything will be okay*, she repeated to herself over and over. *Thwack*. Esi's feet hit the ground. He crouched next to her and placed his hand—hot and sweaty from the ropes—against her forehead. "How's my *shetani* . . . ready to get out?"

Little devil. Esi's nickname for her. Asha managed a weak smile.

"They are sending down a board to lift you out." Esi stared at her, his eyes anxious and worried.

A big shadow covered the light. Bits of rock and dirt crumbled as the board knocked against the sides of the well. Esi reached up and grabbed the board. He lowered it to the ground and laid it flat.

"I'm going to slide the board under you."

Asha nodded. Esi gently lifted her shoulder. Even that slight movement tore a scream from her throat.

"What's going on?" Fara and Yesofu called.

"I think her arm is broken or something," replied Esi.

"It's okay, it's okay, it's okay." Asha pumped herself up as

271

she would before a carrom tournament. "You can do this." She took a deep breath, and then nodded. "Go ahead, Esi. And if . . . if I scream again, just ignore me."

Esi leaned over Asha. "Keep your eyes on me. Now take a deep breath."

Asha filled her lungs with air. In one swift movement, Esi thrust his arms under her, scooped her up, and set her down upon the board. She clenched her teeth to keep from crying out. He leaned over to tie ropes around her legs, torso, and forehead, then looked up. "Pull!"

The board creaked under her weight, but Asha felt it rise up.

"I'm going to climb up alongside you," said Esi.

Asha could hear pulling . . . groaning . . . squeaking coming from above. The board banged against the wall and a stabbing pain shot up Asha's arm.

"You're almost there," said Esi.

The board moved upward, closer and closer to the opening, with Esi holding it steady. Air brushed against her face and neck. She'd be free soon.

"Keep pulling," a voice called out.

Faces . . . many of them . . . stared at her from above, but she locked onto Yesofu and he held her gaze. The board moved up and up. She slid as the board tipped slightly before straightening and sliding into the open.

"We've got her!" Yesofu cried out.

Relief turned Asha limp. She was safe. Yesofu had saved her. "Thank you."

Yesofu grabbed her hand. "I can't believe you came here."

"I had to—"

Yesofu got a funny look on his face that was hard to read. Her relief reflected in his face? Gratitude? Or was it something else?

"I'm so sorry, Asha."

"You have nothing to be sorry about."

A siren screamed in the distance. Fara appeared by Yesofu's side. "They'll be here any minute. Let me cover her." Fara set a blanket over Asha and pressed her lips against her forehead. The lights from the ambulance shined closer. Asha closed her eyes. Lying in the well all those hours with nothing but her thoughts, she realized she was right—it was time to let go . . . of Entebbe and of Yesofu. She'd be leaving soon. To a new life. To a new country. She could no longer think of Entebbe as home. And Yesofu should focus on his life, his friends.

Yesofu intertwined his fingers with Asha's.

She opened her eyes and squeezed his hand.

3 DAYS

52

YESOFU

YESOFU PEERED OVER the top of the hibiscus shrub surrounding the patio. Asha was in her room, sitting up in bed. Her one arm was tied in a sling. The doctor had set her dislocated shoulder after she'd been pulled from the well and taken to the hospital.

"What are you waiting for?" Esi shouted. He sat on his scooter at the bottom of the hill outside the Grade A hospital. "Hurry up!"

Yesofu waved his hand to shush up his brother. He couldn't just barge into Asha's room. He definitely did not want to run into Sister Masani again. But then, Asha looked over, smiled, and waved. Yesofu stepped up to climb over the rail and stopped. If he kept his mouth shut, she'd leave and never know the truth. He bit his lip, thinking what to do. Asha leaned forward, looking at him. But he'd always know. He patted his pocket, making sure the surprise he'd brought her was still inside. Then he leapt over the railing onto the patio and slipped into her room.

"*Habari*," said Asha. "What are you doing here?"

"I got Esi to give me a ride." He shot a quick glance into the corridor.

"You're okay," said Asha. "Mama went home and Sister Masani's at her desk."

Yesofu looked at Asha as he dragged a chair closer to the bed. Of course, she could still tell what he was thinking. He gripped the sides of the chair so tightly that the skin pulled over his knuckles. He had so much he needed to tell her.

"Yesofu," Asha said suddenly.

"Asha," Yesofu said at the same time.

They looked at one another and laughed.

"You first," said Yesofu.

"I wasn't sure I'd see you before we leave," said Asha. "That's why I went to Katabi. I didn't count on running into Akello—"

Yesofu shifted and the chair legs scraped on the tile. "I can't believe he did that. Leaving you in that well . . . that was—"

"But you saved me. I wouldn't be here if it wasn't for you. Forget Akello."

Yesofu looked at Asha smiling at him. He wished he could forget Akello.

Asha stared at him. "What's going on?"

He had to tell her even if it meant she'd hate him.

"It's my fault your papa was arrested," said Yesofu. "I told Akello."

53

ASHA

HIS WORDS CRASHED down upon Asha. Her heart raced so fast it felt like it would rush right out of her chest. Images flashed in her head—Akello inside the soldier's jeep. The smug look on his face.

"I'm so sorry." Yesofu looked at Asha. "I never thought that he'd—"

"What?" Anger gripped Asha and wouldn't let go. "What, Yesofu? You never thought that Akello would figure out it was Papa? That he'd tell? That the soldiers would come to my house and take Papa away?"

"I didn't do it to hurt you or get your dad arrested."

"Then why?" Despite the heat, Asha rubbed the goose

bumps on her arm. "We're supposed to be friends."

"No matter what you think, I never stopped being your friend."

"But you did," Asha said quietly.

Yesofu leaned forward and then fell back in his chair. "I knew you wouldn't understand."

"You're right. I don't."

"It wasn't about you."

"Then who?"

"Me."

Yesofu made no sense. Asha gripped the bedsheet, waiting for him to explain how him telling Akello had nothing to do with her.

"Asha, you're my best friend. But we were never equals, not really. I'm African and that meant I would never be as good as you. It's the way things are . . . or were."

"You could have talked to me." Asha spoke slowly, trying not to show how hurt she felt.

"That's just it," said Yesofu. "With Akello, I didn't have to. He already knew."

"But you never gave me a chance," Asha shot back.

"You're supposed to be my best friend. How come you never asked how I was doing . . . not even once?"

A barrier, like the roadblocks along Entebbe Road, settled between them, and neither said a word. Deep down, Asha knew Yesofu was right. She'd never worked in the sugarcane fields. She'd never drawn water from a well for cooking. She'd never even had to wash her own clothes. Yesofu deserved to have everything she had or used to have. She wished she'd realized sooner how not having these things did make a difference. But still it didn't change what had happened.

Yesofu sat stoop-shouldered and silent.

The clock on the wall ticked, counting the seconds. Minutes.

Asha could see that Yesofu still cared. He didn't have to come here today and tell her the truth, but he did. That had to count for something. If she held on to her anger she'd not only be hurting him, she'd be hurting herself too. And she'd have to live with that for the rest of her life. There'd be no way to forgive him.

Yesofu stood. "I should go." He sounded beaten down, as if all the life had gone out of him.

"I'm sorry."

Asha took a deep breath.

"Me too."

Yesofu looked up, his eyes wide.

"I was selfish. I didn't stop to think how your life was changing too. I didn't ask how you were doing or what was happening. And I should have. I wish I had."

Yesofu didn't sit back down. He didn't walk over to her.

He stood, saying nothing.

Asha waited.

The clock ticked.

Maybe it was too late for sorry. Or maybe the difference between his life and hers was like the divide in the Great Rift Valley—too wide and too big to be bridged.

54

YESOFU

YESOFU LOOKED AT Asha.

"You told me on the night of my birthday party that we were different," she said. "I didn't understand then. But I do now. I never really thought about what your life was like outside my world."

"You're right . . . you are kind of selfish."

Asha sat up too quickly and winced. "Hey!"

Yesofu tried hard not to smile, but the sides of his mouth twitched until he couldn't hold it in any longer. He grinned at her. With her good arm, Asha flung a pillow at him. He ducked and it sailed over his head. At that moment Sister Masani walked in carrying a medical chart. The pillow landed at her feet.

"Time to check your temperature and—" She stopped when she saw Yesofu.

Yesofu moved toward the door and tipped his chair, catching it just in time. "Sister Masani, I w-w-was just . . . I mean, I came to—"

"I think I hear the phone ringing," she said, and spun around on her heel and walked out. "I'm sure Asha will be resting quietly and *alone* when I return," she called from the corridor.

Yesofu picked up the pillow and handed it to Asha.

She gripped it tight, pulling at the seams of the case. "I don't know if I'll see you again."

The realness of everything started to sink in. "When are you leaving for London?"

Asha shook her head. "Canada, not London. *Keep Britain White.* They're like Idi Amin. They don't want us either. Our plane leaves tomorrow."

Canada. That was on the other side of the world. Yesofu reached into his pocket, keeping the surprise hidden in his fist. Then he opened his fingers and held out his hand.

Asha leaned forward, too quickly. "Ow!" She winced. "Those look exactly like my beads . . . the ones from my bracelet. Did you buy new ones?" She pulled Yesofu's hand closer. "Wait. These are mine—aren't they?"

Yesofu nodded.

"But it snapped when I fell into the well."

"Esi saw them and grabbed what he could before he came out," said Yesofu. "That's why there's only four. It's all he could find." He dropped the beads into her hand. "Red for hibiscus flowers. Brown for sweetgrass. Blue for Lake Victoria. And orange for the sunsets." When the last bead dropped, Yesofu closed her fingers.

"Is this goodbye?"

Yesofu shook his head. "*Tutakutana tena*."

"Not goodbye. Until we meet again," Asha repeated.

Yesofu nodded. He didn't know if he'd ever have the chance to leave Uganda, much less get to Canada, but he couldn't begin to believe that this was forever.

They stayed there—hands clasped together—in the soft silence. Then, slowly, Asha's hand slipped out of his. Yesofu took a step back. He tried to make a move to leave, but his feet wouldn't listen. He took a deep breath. "Count to five?"

Asha nodded.

"*Moja*."

"One."

"*Mbili*."

"Two."

"*Tatu*."

"Three." Asha opened her hand. The light from the window caught the beads, sending a burst of color across the hospital room.

"*Nne, tano.*" They finished counting together in Swahili.

"Goodbye, my friend."

"*Kwaheri rafiki yangu.*"

1 DAY

≋ 55 ≋
ASHA

ASHA SAT ALONE in her bedroom. Packing was a lot harder with only one hand, and her sling kept getting in the way. Until the soldiers took Papa away, she didn't think it would really happen. Everyone else had left, but somehow she'd never imagined the day would come when she would have to do the same. The thought of never again waking up in her bedroom, or hearing Fara singing, or running home from the Entebbe Club to Mama's banging on a saucepan, or walking home from school with Yesofu . . . the list went on and on. After tomorrow Asha would never see this house again.

Beyond her bedroom, Asha heard Fara moving about. It was hard to imagine that she'd never again hear the clatter of Fara's footsteps. Mama had told Fara to look through the boxes and take what she wanted. If she didn't, the soldiers would take everything for themselves.

"Asha!" Mama called from downstairs. "Have you finished packing?"

"Almost," Asha replied. She was only allowed one small suitcase, and it lay open on her bed filled with sweaters, long-sleeved shirts, and pants—clothes for the cold weather in Canada. Everything else she was leaving behind. Her favorite *salwar kameez* and statue of Ganesh. The sound of chirping weaverbirds. The sweet scent of the bougainvillea shrubs. None of it was coming with her.

Her eyes fell upon the wooden framed photograph sitting on the edge of her desk. She picked up the frame and looked at the boy and girl in the black-and-white photograph taken last year at Lake Victoria. Papa had taken her and Yesofu fishing that day and they'd caught three huge tilapia.

Asha pulled the photograph out of the frame to take a closer look. The lake was still, and only a few frothy white ripples lapped around the base of the small wooden fishing boat. Asha, in her shorts and cotton tunic, stood perched on her tiptoes, leaning slightly into Yesofu. He held up the three fish in one hand and had his other arm around her shoulders.

"Remember to pack only what is absolutely necessary," Mama called out.

Asha's stomach tightened. The photo was small and flat. She pressed her fingertip against Yesofu's face, and then tucked the photo between two sweaters. Asha closed the suitcase and clicked the metal snaps shut. She paused in the doorway and cast one last look at her bedroom. Ganesh sat on her nightstand. Idi Amin was one obstacle that the elephant god hadn't been able to remove.

Asha picked up her suitcase and walked downstairs. On the table were receipts attached to a declaration of assets form. Mama had to itemize almost everything they owned . . . car, house, jewelry, furniture. They couldn't leave without it. Another form from the Bank of Uganda so Mama could buy their airline tickets. Fifty shillings was all they could take out.

Mama looked up as Asha came into the sitting room. "Ready?"

Asha nodded. Mama wore her orange *salwar kameez*, the one Papa said lit up her face and brightened a room. But today the orange only darkened the circles under her eyes.

"Take your suitcase out to the verandah. I still have to pack a few more things." She hugged Asha, careful to avoid the sling holding her shoulder, and hurried upstairs.

Asha stepped outside. Her neighborhood hadn't felt normal in a long time. It couldn't with nobody walking along the streets or out riding their bikes. Nobody. The silence was so complete that when she lowered her suitcase, the worn wooden planks creaked and she jumped. She glanced at the carrom board. A few days ago, she'd been playing with Papa.

Asha pressed her eyes closed against the pain of missing him.

Fara was in the driveway, opening the hatchback of their neighbor's old car. Mama'd given Papa's car to Esi. Their white Mercedes would attract the soldiers' attention. Fara lifted Asha's suitcase and set it inside the back of the car. Asha sank onto the steps leading onto the verandah and rested her chin in her hands. Fara walked over. Asha said nothing, just shifted slightly to make room for her *ayah*.

"Yesofu came and saw me," Asha whispered.

"I know, *malaika*," said Fara. "Letting go of those we love is never easy."

"I didn't want to," whispered Asha.

"Neither did he."

Fara hugged Asha tightly. She smelled like the lemon soap she used to scrub saucepans. Like *chai* with cloves and cardamom. Asha buried her face in Fara's shoulder, trying to lock in every memory. The door rattled open.

"It's time," said Mama.

Fara squeezed Asha tightly once more before they stood up together.

Mama clasped Fara's hands. *"Asante sana."*

Fara nodded, keeping her eyes lowered. Something shimmered in Fara's hand. A key. It belonged to Mama's jewelry box. "You take this. I hope it'll help."

She looked up. "Thank you."

As Mama walked toward the car, Asha felt Fara's gaze rest

294

upon her. "*Kwaheri, malaika.*" Fara's eyes glazed. "*Ninaku-penda.*"

"Goodbye," said Asha. "I love you too."

Asha crawled into the back seat and squeezed between the suitcases, her legs feeling as heavy as wet cement. She glanced at her bedroom window. The light was on. She wanted to run back in to turn it off, but what was the point? She slumped against the seat. Mama took her place behind the wheel and turned the key. The car shook and the smell of petrol filled the air.

"Ashok—" Mama whispered.

Asha waited, imagining her father's strong, gentle hands turning over his carrom striker.

Finally, Mama shifted the gear and they pulled out of the driveway. Asha turned and glanced back . . . one last time.

56

YESOFU

YESOFU PEDALED TO the fish market, weaving between the tangled mess of cars and buses wrestling for space on the narrow road. Asha would be gone soon. And this time she wasn't coming back, not as far as they knew. The stench of car fumes flooded the air. He sucked in his breath and held it. Up ahead the road curved, and he followed the bend. He was alone now, apart from the odd car. All the other traffic continued to the airport. His shoulders relaxed and he could breathe normally again.

As Yesofu pedaled past the goats and cattle, the smell of burning oil floated past in the wind. A tea stall owner sat along the roadside, frying cassava in metal pots. The smell made his mouth water, and Yesofu wished he had a few extra shillings, but money was tight at home without Mamma and Esi working for Asha's family and hardly any jobs in the fields for Baba. These opportunities that President Amin had talked about seemed to have disappeared with the Indians. Even the loan that Baba'd tried to get had been rejected. Yesofu waved at the tea stall owner. The man lifted his head and smiled.

Mr. Bhatt.

Yesofu wobbled off the road and he almost fell off his bike. What was the Café Nile owner doing frying cassava at a tea stall? He rode over and stopped.

"Surprised to see me?"

Yesofu nodded. "How come you're still here?"

"Why should I leave?" Mr. Bhatt held out a plate. Steam curled off the fried *mhogo* chips. "I have Ugandan citizenship. I have a right to be here. Just like you."

"But what about the soldiers . . . aren't you worried?"

"Ha!" Mr. Bhatt wiped the beads of sweat from his forehead. "What else can they do? They've taken my home, my business, and my money. But they can't get in here." He pointed to his chest. "It may take a couple of years, but there will be another Café Nile."

Yesofu licked the grease off his fingers and set off. It had to take guts to stay when almost every other Indian was leaving, especially knowing you weren't wanted. Idi Amin had promised that once the Indians left, he'd return the country to the people, to Ugandans. Where would that leave Mr. Bhatt?

There was no sign to identify the wooden fish shack. It sat along the edge of the roadside just up from the lake. Yesofu leaned his bike against a tree and made sure he had the money Mamma had given him. Fish was cheaper at the end of the day. Inside, the bloody hunks of king fish, tilapia, and Nile perch lay out on long tables. Flies buzzed. Yesofu picked up a whole tilapia. He looked into the eyes—cloudy and white. Once the Indians left, would the soldiers leave Entebbe? Would the beatings and bullying stop? Or would Idi Amin turn his army on another tribe? His stomach twisted. Yesofu dropped the fish onto the table and ran outside.

He lay up against a tree, taking deep breaths to settle his stomach. The sky rumbled as a jet pierced the clouds, climbing higher into the sky. The noise was so loud it filled all the space around him. Yesofu wondered if Asha was on that plane, as he'd done every time a plane passed overhead this afternoon. A Land Rover pulled up, loaded with camouflage-clad troops. More soldiers from Amin's army.

One of the soldiers had a pair of binoculars hanging around his neck. He held them up to his eyes and looked out toward the lake. The jeep jerked forward and the soldier slipped and fell into his seat with the binoculars bouncing against his chest. Yesofu tried to hide a laugh. The soldier spun around, and the look he gave Yesofu sent a chill down his spine.

It was Akello.

57

ASHA

THE AIRPORT TERMINAL was complete mayhem. Masses of bodies pushed and shoved Asha as she hurried behind Mama through the sea of brown faces—some light, some dark, some in turbans, some with *bindi* dots nestled between their eyebrows.

"*Chalaa, chalaa,*" said Mama. "Hurry up."

The hard edges of suitcases and boxes bumped against her as people lugged their own bags without help from the usual African porters. She recognized some faces from school and town, but nobody met her gaze. Staggering forward, Asha reached for Mama's hand, squeezing it tightly.

"Over there," said Mama, pointing to a large sign, and her steps quickened.

DEPARTING FLIGHTS FOR CANADA AND USA. The bold black letters glared at Asha. A soldier stood just outside the doors, his fingers wrapped tightly around the rifle he held against his chest. She felt his eyes on her as she stepped through the doors. Inside the crowded room, a cacophony of sounds burst on Asha like thunder—shouting, crying, thumping, shrieking. Mama joined one of the queues behind an elderly couple. The husband's gray hair hung below his shoulders, crooked and jagged.

The woman noticed Asha staring. "The soldiers did it." She shook her head. "With a broken bottle," the elderly lady said to Mama. She sliced her hand through the air. "Ripped off his turban and cut off his hair."

Asha set down her suitcase in the line and sat on it. Two officers stood at the front, checking suitcases and stamping passports. Behind the officers, a large window overlooked the runway. A huge plane taxied, waiting to take off. The propellers spun faster and faster as it moved away from the terminal. The engine roared and lifted into the sky.

"Next!" shouted the security officer, waving and pointing at Mama.

A tall soldier stepped forward and tapped the tip of his rifle against one of the long, silver metal tables.

"Come on," said Mama.

A metal table separated Mama and Asha from the security officer. He stood tall and straight, his tan shirt stretched snug across his round stomach.

"Passport." His dark eyes sparked with anger as he waited.

Mama's hand trembled as she placed her passport on the counter.

"How many in your family?" The officer didn't even look at Mama when he spoke; his fingers were too busy flipping through the pages. He reached for the metal stamp, pressing it into the purple ink pad. "How many?"

"Two," said Mama. Her bangles jingled as she pointed to Asha.

The officer's hand froze, holding the stamp inches away from the open passport booklet. He looked up, piercing Mama with his gaze, then moving to Asha.

"No husband?"

"He has a visa for America." Mama's voice faltered. She gripped the edge of her *sari* in her hands. "What can we do? We have to go where they will take us."

Asha felt Mama's fingers close tightly around her arm. She couldn't believe how easily Mama had lied. They waited for the officer to decide. Finally, he banged the stamp in the ink pad.

Thump. A stamp for Mama.

Thump. A stamp for her.

The page was bruised with a dark purple stain. The officer slid the passport across to Mama. "He'll check your suitcases," he said, and pointed to another officer standing next to the baggage ramp.

Mama lifted the suitcases onto the metal table. After passing through six checkpoints along Entebbe Road, what did the officer think he would find? He patted the cuffs and lining of the clothes, pulling and yanking at the hems of tunics, almost ripping off the embroidery and mirrored beads. When he was finished with the last suitcase, he snapped his fingers, and within seconds the two bags disappeared through a dark hole in the wall.

Just as they turned to leave, the officer held up a hand to stop them.

"We're not done."

≋58≋

YESOFU

YESOFU HADN'T SEEN Akello since that night they pulled Asha out of the well. His mamma and two sisters were still in Katabi, but Akello had disappeared. He'd left them just like his dad had done.

"Akello?"

He didn't answer. It was as if he didn't see Yesofu, but then he climbed out of the jeep. He wore the standard army camouflage uniform. Only on Akello, it hung in places, like he didn't quite fit. The beret on his head sat at a crooked angle and slipped lower on his forehead as he walked over. Yesofu stood and matched Akello's stare.

"You joined the army?" Even as Akello stood in front of

him, he still couldn't quite believe that this was his friend. "Why?"

"You wouldn't get it."

"Try me."

"It's just . . . We don't sit around waiting for our dreams to happen. We're doing something to make them happen."

"Like leaving Asha in the well."

"I would have let her out. . . ."

"What about getting her dad arrested?"

"They had Mr. Gomez on their watch list. I didn't tell the soldiers anything they didn't already know."

"But you didn't know that."

"I did what I had to do."

Yesofu couldn't imagine ever needing to do something like that, to betray a friend, put someone in danger. "What happened to you?"

Akello shrugged. "I've got a bed. I don't have to worry about food. I'm doing something for Uganda. How can that be so wrong?"

"Keep telling yourself that . . . but it isn't true."

"Akello!" one of the soldiers shouted from the jeep. "*Harakisha.*"

Akello fell silent. Then he turned and walked back to the jeep.

Yesofu stared at the dust cloud the soldiers left behind.

Yesofu hopped on his bike and headed home, too late

remembering the fish Mamma had asked him to buy. Idi Amin had promised change would come to Uganda. And he was right. Everything had changed. No Asha. No Akello. No jobs. No money for school fees. No food. Dada Amin had promised a great future, but a future is hard to build when there's nothing left.

≋59≋

ASHA

THE OFFICER HELD Mama in his stare. Asha clenched her hands into fists. They were leaving Entebbe. That's what Amin and all these soldiers wanted. Why couldn't they just leave them alone and let them get on the plane? Mama didn't move, except for her fingers, warm and sweaty, as they crept down Asha's arm, searching for her hand. Her gold bangles jingled ever so slightly.

"Hand me your purse," the soldier demanded.

Mama released Asha's hand and placed her purse on the metal table. The officer's eyes were glued to Mama's bangles. He placed his hand inches away from her fingers.

"The money for that gold came from my country," he said. "My people worked so you could afford those."

Mama didn't say anything, but her shoulders slumped, like she couldn't take one more thing. She pressed her arm against her heart and held it there for a minute. Then she looked at the officer and pushed the cluster of bangles together, until they formed one thick band of gold.

Then her fingers reached for one of the bangles, pulling it apart from the group, sliding it down her arm and over her knuckles. She held it in the air, swinging it between her fingers before setting it down in front of the officer.

"What are you doing?" said Asha. "Papa gave those to you."

Mama held up her hand. One by one she slid each thin bangle off her arm and set them down on the metal counter.

Ting.

Ting.

Ting.

The bracelets tinkled against one another as Mama kept adding another and another until all twelve lay in a cluster of gold on the table. When her arm was bare, she stood up straight with her shoulders back.

"Now you can go."

Mama met the officer's gaze, her lips tight against whatever politeness would have been required in some other time. Then she turned and walked out the doors.

Asha stepped outside into a hot gush of wind. She followed Mama out onto the tarmac, where a massive plane waited—a big, white BOAC DC-8. She pressed her fists over her ears to drown out the grinding sound of the giant propellers. The Ugandan flag flapped in the light breeze. Mama climbed onto the first step leading into the plane. Asha reached into her pocket and pulled out the four beads, holding them tightly in her fist. Her eyes scanned the lush mountains and billowing palm trees as the familiar wind cooled her skin. She shut her eyes and she did not see Uganda. She saw Papa's face. Kind and knowing.

Mama took hold of Asha's hand, squeezing it tightly, and Asha opened her eyes, looking through tears. The sun was sinking into the horizon, leaving behind an orangey glow. Neither of them said a word, but in that moment of absolute stillness, Asha knew they were both thinking of him.

Asha took a long, deep breath, and Mama's chest rose and fell in rhythm with hers.

"*Tutakutana tena.*"

Until we meet again.

And together they stepped onto the plane.

90 DAYS IN HISTORY

A Countdown to the Expulsion

In August 1972, President Idi Amin announced that there was no room in Uganda for Indians, spurring thousands of people to flee their homes. Here is what happened in the days leading up to the deadline:

August 4   President Idi Amin announces that all Indians with British citizenship have 90 days to leave Uganda.

August 6   India refuses to allow fifty thousand Indians with British citizenship to enter India, claiming that they are primarily Britain's responsibility.

August 7   President Amin amends his announcement, expanding the expulsion to include all Indians with foreign citizenship.

August 8   Kenya closes its borders to any Indians leaving Uganda.

August 11   Indians in Uganda must now request approval from the Central bank to take any money out of the country.

August 12   Britain sends a government representative to

Kampala, the capital of Uganda, to convince President Amin to allow Indians to stay.

August 13   After failing to persuade President Amin, Britain decides to admit up to fifty thousand Indians from Uganda, if they are also British citizens.

Britain requests help from countries in the United Nations in taking in Indian refugees.

August 14   President Amin declares that all Indians with Ugandan citizenship who do not verify their papers at the Immigration Office by September 10 will automatically lose their claims of Ugandan citizenship.

August 20   President Amin extends the expulsion to include all eighty thousand Indians in Uganda, including the twenty-three thousand who thought they had Ugandan citizenship.

August 22   The United Nations steps in under the Human Right's Declaration to help the twenty-three thousand Indians without citizenship in any country to find refuge in other countries.

August 26   Canada sends a team of immigration officials to Uganda to accelerate the processing of applications from Indians wishing to come to

Canada. Prime Minister Pierre Trudeau says Canada is likely to take up to five thousand refugees.

August 27 President Amin announces that he will seize all foreign-owned businesses in Uganda.

August 31 The first group of refugees to leave Uganda arrives in London.

September 1 President Amin aims to make Uganda economically independent by not allowing any Ugandan shillings to leave the country.

September 4 The United Kingdom asks an additional fifty countries to accept expelled Ugandan Indians.

September 28 Canada accepts its first group of Indian refugees leaving Uganda.

October 3 The United States agrees to accept one thousand Asian Ugandans who are stateless—not recognized as a citizen of any other country.

October 17 President Amin announces that Indians will face up to two years' imprisonment and a fine of fifty thousand shillings if they attempt to sell their business privately before they leave instead of turning it over to the government.

November 1 The United Nations agrees to fly out the four thousand Indians without any citizenship by the November 8 deadline and place them in transit camps before final resettlement in Europe and overseas.

November 8   Malta, Morocco, Greece, and Spain offer to help evacuate two thousand refugees from Uganda on the final day before the deadline, with assistance from the Red Cross.

November 9   The ninety-day period for Indians to leave Uganda ends.

Idi Amin decrees that all Indians still in Uganda are required to be registered. Less than eight hundred Indians are still in Uganda and most of these either have Ugandan citizenship or are expatriates from countries other than the United Kingdom.

AUTHOR'S NOTE

Some of the details in this story have been fictionalized, but the major events are based on research, news articles, interviews with family and friends, as well as my own memories. Though I was born in Entebbe, I left with my father and mother for Britain shortly after Idi Amin seized control of the presidency. In the weeks leading up to the expulsion deadline, I remember the family and friends who arrived on our doorstep in London, like my Aunty Phina and her three children. Over the years, I learned more about the expulsion through the stories told at gatherings and reunions. Stories about how disbelief and denial quickly turned to fear as violence, torture, and murder spread throughout Uganda. How homes and businesses were lost. How families were separated in a rush to leave before the deadline. Seeking to understand why the expulsion took place and what it has meant to Uganda, I researched events leading up to the expulsion and spoke to both African Ugandans and Indians.

The roots of the expulsion go back to 1895, when the Imperial British Government recruited Indian laborers to work on the construction of the railway line. After the completion of the railway in the twentieth century, some of these workers returned home to India, while others chose to stay. Over time, those who remained took up different jobs in other fields. While Uganda was still under British rule, a social system emerged that separated classes by ethnicity— Europeans, then Indians, and then Africans—affecting salaries, education, and social communities. In 1962, when President Milton Obote led Uganda into independence from Britain, Africans saw very little change in their status or quality of life, while Indians saw an increase in job and business opportunities. With growing concerns that Indians were monopolizing businesses and employment, many Africans in Uganda began to feel increased resentment toward Indians. By 1970, Africans had started placing pressure on the government to reduce the number of Indians in Uganda. And in response to this pressure, Obote's government pursued a policy of "Africanization," which targeted Ugandan Indians by restricting the role of non-citizen Indians in economic and professional activities.

In 1971, the commander of the army, Idi Amin, launched a military coup overthrowing Obote. He then declared himself president of Uganda and significantly increased the policies toward Africanization. He set up the State Research Bureau and Public Safety Unit, a military intelligence agency with the main purpose of eliminating those who opposed his regime. To further secure his position of power,

Amin then declared an "economic war" aimed at transferring the economic control of Uganda back into the hands of Africans. This included a set of policies that seized properties owned by Asians and Europeans. In August 1971, Amin ordered a review of Indian citizenships and canceled any outstanding applications. In early December, he convened an Indian Conference where he acknowledged the Indians' contributions to the economy and various professions, but also accused them of disloyalty, non-integration, and commercial malpractice.

On August 4, 1972, President Idi Amin ordered the expulsion of the fifty thousand Indians with British passports within ninety days. This was later amended to include all sixty thousand Indians who were not Ugandan citizens. By the time of the deadline, around thirty thousand Ugandan Asians immigrated to the UK. Others went to Commonwealth countries such as Australia, South Africa, Canada, and Fiji, or to India, Kenya, Sweden, Tanzania, and the United States.

In the years following the expulsion, Amin continued to seize businesses and properties that had belonged to Indians and Europeans and give them to his supporters. These businesses were mismanaged, which contributed to the further decline of Uganda's economy. Inflation was around 200 percent a year and basic necessities like sugar, salt, and cooking oil soon became available only on the black market.

Idi Amin's brutality and widespread killings continued through his eight years in control. His victims included members of other ethnic groups, as well as religious leaders, judges, lawyers, students, intellectuals, criminal suspects, and foreign nationals. Among the most prominent people killed were: Benedicto Kiwanuka, the first prime minister of Uganda; Janani Luwum, the archbishop of the Church of Uganda; Joseph Mubiru, the former governor of the Bank of Uganda; Frank Kalimuzo, the vice chancellor of Makerere University; and two of Amin's own cabinet ministers, Erinayo Wilson Oryema and Charles Oboth Ofumbi. The exact number of people killed is unknown, but exile organizations, with the help of Amnesty International, estimate that the number is around 500,000, marking Idi Amin as one of the most brutal military dictators to wield power in post-independence Africa. Today, the nation is still rebuilding its economy, but many Africans now own and manage schools, universities, hospitals, shops, resorts, and large enterprises.

Asha and Yesofu are both fictional, reflecting my own experiences and understanding of Uganda. Their story embodies tragedy, hope, and the strength of the human spirit in the face of adversity. But more than anything, I wanted the significance of their friendship to shine through. In all the stories I heard growing up and the times I saw family and friends meet—some for the first time since

318

leaving Uganda—I noticed the most powerful connection was knowing who will be there for you, no matter what or when. And, I came to realize that no matter how many years passed since everyone had seen one another, the strong bonds of friendship and love that had been cultivated in Uganda endured.

Entebbe Institute gathering, circa 1952. Third row: Daddy's younger brother is sitting on Papa's lap and Nana is standing to his left.

Mum and me in our garden in Entebbe, circa 1969. Mum worked at the Grade A hospital and had delivered one of Idi Amin's sons when he was still in the army.

Daddy and me in the Botanical Gardens, circa 1970.

Kampala Institute Jubilee Celebration, circa 1960. Daddy was on the planning committee and is standing next to his future sister-in-law, reviewing his speech.

BIBLIOGRAPHY

"Country Studies: Uganda: Post-Independence Security Services." Federal Research Division. United States Library of Congress.

"Disappearances and Political Killings—Human Rights Crisis of the 1990s—A Manual for Action." Amsterdam: Amnesty International, 1994.

"Flight of the Asians," *Time*. September 11, 1972.

Honey, Martha and Ottaway, David B. "Idi Amin Squandered the Wealth of Uganda." *The Washington Post*, May 29, 1979.

Keatley, Patrick. "Obituary: Idi Amin." *The Guardian* (UK edition), August 18, 2003.

Lubwama, Siraje K and Abdullah, Halima. "Who Were Amin's Victims?" Daily Monitor Special Report. Uganda. August 20, 2003. Retrieved from www.monitor.co.ug.

Luganda, Patrick. "Amin's Economic War Left Uganda on Crutches." New Vision. Kampala. July 29, 2003.

Patel, Hasu H. "General Amin and the Indian Exodus from Uganda." *A Journal of Opinion*. 1972.

ADDITIONAL RESOURCES

Fiction

- *Child of Dandelions* by Shenaaz Nanji
- *Where the Air Is Sweet* by Tasneem Jamal

Nonfiction

- *Out of Uganda in 90 Days* by Urmila Patel
- *RSVP Rice and Stew Very Plenty: The Story of an Ismaili Girl's Expulsion from Uganda and Acceptance in Canada* by Nazlin Rahemtulla with Margaret Fairweather

Films

- *Mississippi Masala*
- *The Last King of Scotland*
- *Amin: the Rise and Fall*

ACKNOWLEDGMENTS

Feeling gratitude and not expressing it
is like wrapping a present and not giving it.
—*William Arthur Ward*

Thanks to . . .

—the family and friends who trusted me with their personal stories and experiences.

—Uma Krishnaswami, Sarah Aronson, and Kim Griswell for sharing their expertise and support.

—SCBWI for the work-in-progress grant that motivated me to persevere.

—Louise and Trixie for reading earlier versions and planting seeds of inspiration.

—the Kampala and Entebbe Goan Institutes for permission to use the photographs.

—Rebecca Aronson for taking a chance on this story and joining me on a path of *firsts*—first acquisition for an editor and first novel for a writer. You are incredible.

—Mabel Hsu and the team at Katherine Tegen Books for embracing this story and designing a brilliant book.

—the families and people affected by Idi Amin's expulsion order. I am in awe of how you persevered in the face of adversity. He forced you to leave everything, but he couldn't take away your determination, resilience, and spirit for life. Thank you for allowing me to tell your story.

And finally . . .

—the biggest thanks to my husband and daughter for your unwavering support.